Locked

(The Alpha Group Trilogy #1)

Maya Cross

This book is a work of fiction, the characters, incidents and dialogues are products of the author's imagination and are not to be construed as real.

Publisher: Maya Cross via Createspace
City: Sydney

ISBN-13: 978-1484021958

Dedicated to C.
For putting up with an awful lot.

Chapter 1

It was nearly one in the morning when I realised that I was about to do something stupid. Ordinarily, I'm not someone who is prone to random acts of mischief. By day I'm as straight as they come. But get a few glasses of red into me, and suddenly that little devil on my shoulder starts sounding a whole lot more reasonable.

And tonight was definitely one of those nights.

I was sitting in a shabby little bar with two friends, celebrating Louisa's engagement. We'd only been there an hour, but the empty glasses were already starting to accrue in embarrassing amounts on the table in front of us. Our attention was focused on a finely dressed couple who were walking through a doorway at the back of the room.

"My money's on...international drug lord," I said.

"I'm going to go with local mafia," Louisa replied. We both looked expectantly at Ruth.

"Billionaire men's underwear mogul!" the other woman declared grandly, swaying a little in her seat. The three of us dissolved into giggles.

We were no strangers to a drink or two on a weeknight, but given that it was a special occasion, we'd wanted to take it up a notch. I'm not sure who actually uttered the words 'pub crawl', but all that mattered was it was said. Before I knew what was happening, we'd set off on a merry trek around Sydney. Five hours and four bars later, I was well on the way towards a killer hangover.

The bar we were in was not one of our usual haunts, and for good reason. It was the sort of place that might kindly have been described as 'a renovators dream,' or 'full of character.' In other words, it was a bit of a shit-hole. The angular metal tables looked like they'd been dug from some Soviet Cold War bunker, and the floor sloped away dangerously to one side, as though some of the foundations had simply given up and headed for greener pastures. The only wine they sold was a rather dubious house red, and it came served in the same squat, slightly grimy tumblers as every other drink on the menu.

If it'd been a normal night out, we'd never have considered visiting a place like this. It certainly didn't look like the kind of establishment that would be particularly friendly towards a couple of high spirited, professional women out on a bender. But the booze that was swilling around in our stomachs made us bold, and rather than continuing on our way, we'd found ourselves giggling and making a beeline for the entrance.

In retrospect I was rather glad we did, because there was something intriguing about the place, something that wasn't evident from first glance. Most of the other patrons were what I'd expected; sullen, rough looking, and wearing tradesman's clothes, they eyed us over their foaming cups with a kind of resentful curiosity. But shortly after we'd arrived, an unobtrusive doorway on the rear wall had opened, and a security guard had taken up position in front. Gradually, new people began to trickle in and disappear into the back, people that clearly didn't belong in a dump like this. None of the regulars seemed to care, but that little mystery had set my mind wandering.

"What about the girl?" Louisa asked.

Ruth snorted. "Professional trophy wife?"

"With a Ph.D in Pilates," I added.

"Who also happens to be the next Elizabeth Taylor, if only someone would give her a chance," Ruth finished.

Louisa chuckled. "We're such bitches. For all we know she could be perfectly lovely. It's probably a bloody banking conference or something."

I shook my head. "Bankers don't meet in strange rooms up the back of no name bars." My eyes were firmly fixed on the doorway now. To the casual observer, it might have looked unremarkable — just your everyday corporate gathering — but something about the whole situation struck me as strange. Maybe it was just the alcohol catching up with me, I don't know, but my curiosity was piqued.

None of the bartenders were any help. All they'd say was it was a private function. I couldn't even get a company name out of them. It didn't make any sense. Who were these people that their meeting was such a secret? And why hide it away back here in this place?

"Well, unless you plan on flashing the guard a peek at the girls so we can sneak in, I doubt we'll ever know," Ruth said.

"Don't give her ideas," Louisa replied, now staring at me. "She's got that look in her eyes again."

"What look?" I asked.

"The look that says, 'I'm preparing to make a giant, drunken ass of myself again.'"

"Now when have I ever done that?" I replied, unable to contain my grin. In truth, I did have something of a history of getting a little crazy on big nights out. Being a lawyer is hard work. Eighty hour weeks, mounds of paperwork, Partners constantly hounding you; half the time I felt like a worn guitar string that was just a few strums away from snapping. So on those rare occasions that I did get some R&R, I tended to cut loose more than I should. It felt good to just put Professional Sophia in a box for a few hours and forget about her.

Louisa didn't look amused. "Come on Soph, why ruin a perfectly good night by getting yourself kicked out?"

"I haven't said I'm doing anything yet!"

"But you're thinking about it."

My grin widened. "Maybe."

Louisa sighed. "One of these days you're going to get yourself into actual trouble, you know."

The sensible part of me agreed with her. It wasn't exactly lawyerly to be getting tossed out into the street on my ass at one in the morning. But on the other hand, the situation was rather mysterious, and my brain had been marinating in alcohol for hours. I felt restless, energetic, daring; daring enough to do something I might regret later.

I watched as another couple slipped casually into the bar and headed for the back. Whoever these people were, they might as well have had dollar signs printed on their foreheads. Armani, Gucci, Louis Vuitton, Prada; it was like Milan Fashion Week.

Most of the visitors were men. Suited and broad shouldered, they all exuded that kind of arrogant confidence that comes from a lifetime of getting exactly what you want. Some had partners on their arms as well; slim, rouged, perfectly varnished girls, many of whom looked barely out of high school. By glossy magazine standards they were probably attractive, but to me they just looked fake, more like ornaments than real people.

"Come on," I said, "where's your sense of adventure?"

4

"I'd hardly classify sneaking into some la-di-da business function as an adventure," Louisa replied.

"Hey, if she wants to try, I say let her," Ruth said. "Who knows, maybe she can bring back a couple of the suits for us. There were a few I wouldn't kick out of bed."

"A lot of good that'll do me," Louisa said, pointing to her ring.

"Hey, what he doesn't know can't hurt him," Ruth replied. "It can be like... Soph's engagement present to you. A little bon voyage to the single life!"

I couldn't help but grin at Louisa's indignant expression. Sometimes, I still wondered how we were such a tight group. Louisa was as reserved as Ruth was free spirited, and I worked too hard to be much of either. But nonetheless we'd been friends since university. Somehow, we just clicked.

"I haven't been single for four years," Louisa said.

Ruth giggled. "Oh lighten up Lou, I'm just messing around. Obviously they'll both be for me."

At that moment, the front door of the bar opened, and another sharply dressed man walked in. It took me a few moments to realise that I recognised him.

"No way," I said, my eyes flicking to my friends. They were both staring at him as he crossed the room, mouths hanging slightly open. After a quiet word to the guard, he vanished into the back.

"Did one of you spike this with a little something extra when I wasn't looking?" Ruth asked, glancing down at her drink. "Because I swear that was Chase Adams."

Chase Adams was one of the biggest stars in Hollywood. A home grown Australian hero, he'd had a string of high profile hits in recent years, although he was known more for his washboard abs, axe-blade jaw, and baby blue eyes than any kind of real acting talent. I'm not really the sort of girl who lusts after celebrities, but his presence made things even more interesting. Before, I'd assumed the event was something corporate, but now, I didn't know what to think. None of the other guests had been familiar. Were they minor celebrities I just didn't recognise? Or perhaps Chase was just there as a friend? My head was swimming with a million questions.

"Nope," Louisa said, "I saw him too." She gave her lips a little involuntary lick. "No date either."

"Such a pity you're not single anymore, hey?" Ruth replied with a smirk.

Louisa shot her a withering look, but she couldn't maintain it long.

"So Lou," I said, "still not even a tiny bit curious?"

She glanced at the doorway once more and then sighed. "Maybe a little. But that doesn't change the fact that it's crazy to try and do anything about it." She nodded at the gargantuan man who stood guard in front of the door. "That guy looks like he eats a bowl of nails for breakfast each morning. We're not going to just giggle and bat our eyelashes past him."

I glanced over once more, sizing him up. She had a point. He looked like a secret service agent from some sort of presidential thriller movie. Clean shaven and unsmiling, his barrel chest and tree trunk arms filled the doorway. In stereotypical elite security fashion, his eyes were hidden behind a pair of dark wraparound glasses which looked vaguely ridiculous given the late hour. The coil of an earpiece dangled down one side of his jacket, and every few minutes he'd reach up and press on it, whispering furtively for a moment. Reporting in with the boss, probably.

And all of a sudden, a plan began to take shape in my head.

"Probably not, but maybe I can do one better," I replied. Without giving my brain time to object, I scooped up my drink and stood. I knew it was foolish, but my curiosity was almost overpowering now. I had to know what was going on back there. "Either of you coming?"

Louisa stared up at me like I'd lost my mind, but Ruth merely looked amused. "I think I'd rather just watch," she said, clearly certain that I was about to make a massive fool of myself. I wasn't entirely sure she was wrong. My plan was thin at best. But with a more than healthy dose of Dutch courage circulating inside me, I didn't really care. I was going through that door or getting kicked out in the process.

"Alright then. Let me show you how it's done girls."

And with that, I turned and began marching across the room.

I was basically the perfect level of drunk. Blissful, carefree, a little giddy, but not so far gone that I was slurring or staggering. But the guard didn't know that. The closer I got to him, the more I played it up. As his head turned my way, I threw up a vapid smile and began to stumble a little, gazing around the room in inebriated wonder.

The drunken flirt had gotten me past more than one lengthy club queue in my youth. Don't get me wrong, I don't consider myself to be a knockout or anything – I'd kill for a few more inches of leg, and skin that tanned instead of cooked – but I have certain assets that when emphasised, draw men's eyes nonetheless. The right kind of skirt, a few strategically unfastened buttons, and the rest is usually easy. Unfortunately, Louisa was right; it was going to take more than a smile and a little cleavage to make it through Mr Serious. But I had a special twist in mind for him.

As I arrived in front of the guard, I rocked backwards on my heels, blinking rapidly, as though spotting him for the first time. "Well hello handsome," I said in my best drunken drawl.

The man's lips tightened. "Miss, I'm sorry but this is a private area."

I giggled and batted my eyelashes. "Oh come on now, I just want to talk. Doesn't it get lonely just standing here by yourself all night?"

"I'm fine, but Miss please, I need to keep the doorway clear."

I pondered this for a few seconds. "Well then, I have an idea. How about you come and join me for a drink over there. You can watch your little door sitting down, and I won't be in the way anymore!"

He stared down at me, unblinking and stony faced. "Miss, I'm sorry, but I'm on duty. Please return to your table."

My stomach tightened. I'd been planning on playing it more slowly, but he obviously wasn't in the mood to chat. It was now or never. "Surely you get a break?" I said, leaning closer to brush his arm. "Even a man like you needs a—oh god I'm so sorry!"

He uttered something sharp and flinched backwards, a red stain already blossoming on his chest. I gaped up at him.

"I've ruined your shirt." Setting my now empty wine glass on a nearby table, I reached for some napkins. "I've always been so clumsy. I can't seem to go a day without spilling something. Here, let me clean you up."

As I talked, my eyes flicked to the small plastic receiver that was clipped to his breast pocket. I knew enough about security equipment to know that most earpieces had one. It sent and received signals from the main hub. The question was, had I hit it? In the dim light of the bar it was hard to tell.

I stepped closer to dab his shirt, hoping to get a better look, but he caught my arms in one strong hand. "You've done enough," he said, all politeness gone from his voice. "It's time for you to leave."

He raised his hands to his ear. "Command, this is Jones. I've got a situation here." Seconds passed and nothing happened. He began to look worried. "Command? Hello?" A few more seconds. "Fuck!"

Jackpot.

Now came the real test. He glared down at me, seemingly unsure what to do. As far as I could see, he had two choices. He could wait there until someone came to find out why he'd dropped off the grid, or he could duck inside quickly to let them know there was a problem. Both options had their risks. I was banking on him choosing the latter.

But first, I had to convince him to let me throw myself out. I tried my best to look harmless and afraid, which wasn't difficult. He was an incredibly intimidating man, and his grip felt like a vice around my wrists. *What if I've already gone too far? What if I've bitten off more than I can chew?* I closed my eyes briefly and tried not to panic.

"Okay, okay, I'm sorry. I'll go," I said, keeping my voice meek.

He weighed this up momentarily. "I don't want to see you here again," he said, nodding to the bar.

"No sir."

"I'm going to go clean up, and when I come back, I expect to see you gone."

"No problem."

"Good." He released me.

Giving him one last apologetic smile, I turned and tottered off across the room, breathing a sigh of relief. So far so good.

The front door itself couldn't be seen from his vantage. The bar hooked around ninety degrees at one end, with the exit around the corner. Assuming he stayed put, I could hide there without actually leaving.

It was difficult to resist the urge to look back. I could feel his eyes following me as I walked.

Rounding the corner, I finally let the act drop. Throwing my elbow on the bar, I closed my eyes and sucked in several deep breaths. Even though everything had gone to plan, the whole experience had been decidedly more nerve wracking than I'd expected. Blood was roaring in my ears and I could still feel the buzz of adrenaline coursing through my veins. I briefly debated giving up. People that hired security like that typically did it for a reason; they didn't want to be disturbed. But most of the hard work was already done, and besides, the thought of trudging back to the table and seeing Louisa's snide smile was a little too much to bear at that moment.

Hiding as best I could behind a rack of glasses, I leaned back around the corner and peeked up over the bar. The guard was still at his post, looking conflicted. He cast his eyes around the room, weighing his options. If his employers were looking for privacy, they'd chosen a great location. Even when we'd arrived, the bar had contained less than twenty people, and now in the wee hours of the morning, that number had dwindled considerably. The few remaining patrons were huddled in bleary eyed groups, engrossed in soft conversation. None seemed to be paying much attention to what was going on up the back. It wasn't exactly a high risk situation.

Still, he took his time. *Go on you bastard. Do it.* And after an agonising few seconds, he did. Giving the room one final scan, he spun and marched through the doorway.

I had to restrain myself from cheering. *Not there yet. Now you actually have to get in.* I counted to three slowly in my head, and began walking casually back the way I'd come. Nobody in the room paid me any mind. Catching the girls' eyes, I flashed a triumphant smile. Ruth laughed and stuck up her thumb.

Pausing at the doorway, I took one last look around the room, sucked in a deep breath, and walked through.

Chapter 2

Rather than opening directly into another room, the doorway led to a long passage that ran for sixty feet or so and then hooked off to the right. I reflexively pressed myself against the wall as I caught sight of the guard disappearing around the far corner. Thankfully, he didn't look back.

There was a low buzz emanating from the other end of the corridor. It grew steadily louder the closer I got. Since the door had opened, we'd witnessed maybe two dozen people let through. It was a decent sized group, but not nearly enough to make that sort of noise. I had no idea what it meant.

For the last hour, I'd been trying to picture what lay hidden back there. I'd conjured images of exclusive restaurants and secret board rooms. But nothing prepared me for the reality of what was around the bend.

I turned the corner, and stopped dead in my tracks, my eyes darting left and right, madly trying to take in everything that lay before me. The entire place reeked of decadence. If you took away all the trappings, it *was* basically just a function room, but it was the most lavish function I'd ever seen. The space was far longer than I'd expected; over two hundred feet of polished wood, lush curtains and decorative brass. To one side lay a long redwood bar, laden with more varieties of liquor than I could count. To the other sat circles of high-backed lounges, most of which were filled with suited men, laughing and chatting and swilling drinks. The whole room smelled of malt and cologne and the sharp, earthy scent of leather. There was enough testosterone in the air to corrupt a nunnery.

What really took me by surprise however, was the pool that wove its way up the centre of the room. It was a beautiful sight. Elegantly curved and bathed in colour, it shimmered under a dizzying array of shifting lights that shone down from the roof above.

As I'd suspected, there were far more people present than we'd seen enter. At least a hundred. But where the hell had they all come from? Obviously there had to be other entrances, but why not just come in the front? The whole situation was getting stranger by the minute.

It seemed that whatever the men were discussing, the girls weren't welcome. Most were making good use of the pool, either swimming or lazing on sun chairs to the side, chatting in little groups. A few of them cast eyes my way, like hopefuls at a casting call sizing up their competition. *Relax girls, I'm just visiting.*

As I scanned the room, I spotted several more security personnel posted along the walls. With their dark glasses, it was impossible to tell what they were looking at. At least one was talking into his earpiece, but nobody appeared to be moving towards me. Still, I knew I had to blend in fast.

Unfortunately, the whole place was so overwhelming that I had no idea what to do next. I couldn't see Chase anywhere, and even if I had, I wasn't sure what help that would be. It wasn't like I could just wander up and say hi. I was in over my head. To be honest, I don't think I'd really expected to make it that far. In the heat of the moment, the only plan that sprang to mind was, 'don't get caught.'

So, operating purely on instinct, I headed for the bar. I knew more drink was probably not the wisest move, but it was the most inconspicuous action I could think of, and it would buy me a little time.

"Champagne please," I said to one of the girls behind the counter, doing my best to look at ease.

"Of course. Would you like to see the full list? Otherwise I can recommend a few things. The Dom Perignon ninety-five, the Bollinger ninety-eight and the Krug eighty-eight are all drinking wonderfully at the moment."

I paused, before breaking into a laugh. *What did you expect girl, a ten dollar Prosecco?*

I opened my mouth to respond, but a voice cut in from a little way up the bar. "She'll have a glass of the Krug thanks Amber. And I'll take another Laphroaig. Neat." The man turned his attention to me. "The Krug is lovely. Dry, fruity, but with a hint of sweetness too. And the smell is to die for. I think you'll like it."

As he spoke, he rose and casually moved over to sit next to me. It wasn't my first rodeo. I knew when a man was making a move. And as much as his presumptuousness would normally have annoyed me, I found it difficult to muster much anger. He was gorgeous; a tall, lithe body wrapped in a crisp, charcoal three-piece suit. There's something so god damn sexy about a man who's confident enough to wear a three-piece. It's sophisticated, but with just the right amount of old school charm.

I cast my eyes over him unashamedly, taking in the breadth of his shoulders, the strength of his hands, the way his jacket pulled tight over the powerful curves of his chest. He looked like he'd walked in directly from the set of a Hugo Boss advertisement. My pulse quickened once more.

As I studied him, he stared back, an odd smile playing on his lips. He was older than me, but not old, maybe early thirties, and he had the kind of dark complexion that always set my stomach tingling. That perfect, tantalising combination of olive skin, rugged stubble, and black, unruly hair. However, it was his eyes that really took me down for the count. Sharp and forest-green, they managed to be playful yet incredibly intense. I felt strangely powerless beneath that gaze, like he wasn't just looking at me, but into me. It wasn't fair for a man to have eyes like that.

Eventually, he glanced away, breaking the spell. As my brain kicked back into gear, I was annoyed to find myself adjusting my top. *Come on Sophia, get a grip. He's hardly the first attractive guy who's ever hit on you.* I placed my hands purposefully back on the bar, trying my best not to blush.

"And how would you know what I like?" I asked, adding a little venom to my voice. I hated being taken off balance like that.

"Oh, I don't know. Call it...men's intuition."

I rolled my eyes. "In my experience, men's intuition is rarely as good as they think it is."

He laughed, a look of mock offence appearing on his face. "You'll just have to wait and see won't you?"

His voice was deep and melodic, with hints of an accent; a faint European lilt that I couldn't quite place. It sent a shiver up my spine. I really wanted to be annoyed — that sort of aggressive approach was usually a major turn off for me — but he was making it very difficult.

"I'm Sebastian," he said, offering his hand.

"Sophia," I replied, returning the gesture. His grip was firm, his hand surprisingly rough, and it lingered a little longer than I'd expected.

"What a lovely name."

"It does the job," I said slowly.

He nodded, but said nothing else, seemingly happy to simply sit and study me. "Well Sebastian," I said eventually, feeling strangely self-conscious in the silence, "do you normally approach random girls in bars and select their drinks for them?"

His smile widened. "Quite often, yes."

"And how does that work out for you?"

"It usually has the desired effect."

I laughed. "Oh, and what might that be?"

"A gentleman doesn't kiss and tell," he replied, in a way that did just that. I felt a brief flash of desire at the suggestion, but quickly smothered it. Sure he was attractive, but I wasn't there to become some CEO's trophy lay for the night.

I knew that this was a golden opportunity to find out who these people were, but slightly impaired as I was, I was struggling to find an opening. It didn't help that Sebastian had me completely on the back foot. At first glance he seemed confident and charming, the sort of guy I saw every day around the office. But behind that roguish charisma lay something dangerously alluring; a potent strength that seemed to beckon to my very core. It was intimidating, arousing, and more than a little distracting.

At that moment the waitress arrived, Champagne and scotch in hand.

"Allow me," Sebastian said, taking the bottle and popping the cork with one easy twist of his wrist. He somehow managed to make even that simple gesture look sensual.

As he leaned in to pour, I couldn't help but breathe in the scent of him; scotch and sweat and something much more carnal. He smelled like pure sex, like raw, distilled masculinity. It sucked the breath from my lungs and turned my insides to jelly.

The Champagne fizzed and bubbled as it hit the glass, bringing me back to my senses.

"To men's intuition," he said, handing me the flute and raising his glass. I lifted my own, but refused to acknowledge his toast or the smug smile behind it.

Irritatingly, he was right. The Champagne was amazing. I tried my best to look unimpressed, although I didn't waste much time before taking another sip.

"How is it?" he asked.

I raised my hand and wobbled it from side to side. "It's okay."

His grin said he wasn't fooled, but he played along. "That's a shame. Hopefully next time I can do a better job of pleasing you."

Something about the way he said it made me think he wasn't talking about drinks anymore.

"So Sebastian," I said, desperate to distract myself from the growing warmth between my legs, "when you're not accosting women at parties, what is it you do?"

"I work for Fraiser Capital. We're a venture capital firm. This is actually our gathering here. We throw these every now and again; little meet and greets for some of our clients."

"Ah of course," I said, trying to act like I recognised the name. We were in dangerous territory now. I still wasn't sure how much I was expected to know, or what kind of cover story I needed. I had to tread carefully.

I glanced around the room. "I didn't realise venture capitalists had this kind of money."

"Good ones do."

It seemed a little farfetched to me. The sort of excess on display seemed beyond any sort of corporate gathering. And that didn't explain what the hell Chase Adams was doing there. But pushing any more seemed like a good way to give myself away. "I see. And what makes a good venture capital-ist?"

"The ability to know something special when you see it," he replied, staring directly into my eyes.

I couldn't help but smile at that. I had to hand it to him; he was incredibly smooth. But as much as it was pushing my buttons, I didn't want to give him the satisfaction. I knew how men like him worked. The Partners at my office were no different. It was like a sport to them; dangle a platinum AmEx in the air and watch the ladies flock. I'd even fallen for it a few times in my younger years; it's surprisingly easy to confuse other emotions for love when you don't know any better. Several horrible experiences later, I'd promised myself I'd never be one of those women again.

As if on cue, at that moment, a bikini clad girl appeared at his side.

"There you are, sir," she said, laying a hand on his arm. "I've been looking for you everywhere."

The look she shot me suggested she wasn't pleased about where she'd found him. A girlfriend perhaps? That certainly cast things in a new light.

She was pretty, albeit in a strange, childlike way. Thin, almost frail looking, she had straw blond hair and huge doe eyes that made her seem younger than she probably was.

Sebastian's smile wavered. "Hannah," he said, a hint of displeasure in his voice. "What have I told you about inter-rupting me?"

She balked at his tone, but decided to press on. "Oh, I'm sorry, sir. I just thought you might want to come for a swim with me. The water is lovely."

It didn't take her long to realise she'd made a mistake. In the steely silence that followed, her enthusiasm quickly melted away. It wasn't that Sebastian looked angry — in fact his expression never wavered — but nonetheless I felt something shift in the air, some dangerous charge that hadn't been there before. I knew without it being said that a line had been crossed. Judging by the way Hannah began shrinking into herself, she knew as well.

"It would be rather rude of me to abandon my new friend here in the middle of our conversation, don't you think?" He didn't raise his voice, but there was an edge to it now that said he expected to be agreed with.

It seemed to have the desired effect. Hannah visibly wilted. "Of course sir. You're right. I'm sorry I bothered you."

He nodded in acceptance. There was something strange about the exchange. I'd revised my earlier guess. The way he scolded her didn't make them feel like a couple. But what then? Colleagues? A younger sister maybe? I wasn't sure.

Now that he'd made himself clear, Hannah seemed eager to be anywhere else. Turning quickly without another word, she began heading back towards the pool. For a second I thought that would be the end of it, but just before she disappeared into the crowd, Sebastian called out to her. "And Hannah." She turned, a look of dread on her face. "We'll talk about this later." Hannah nodded slowly.

Watching the defeated girl trudge away, I couldn't help but feel a little sorry for her. I hoped I hadn't gotten her in any real trouble. His reaction seemed a little extreme, given the circumstances.

"I'm sorry about that," he said. "My secretary."

Secretary? Wow, that must be some work environment.

"It's fine. Really, I don't mind," I replied. "Go and have a swim if you want. I'm a big girl; I can take care of myself."

"I'm sure you can, but don't worry. Hannah and I will find time to have a paddle later." His eyes twinkled as he said that, like he'd just told a joke nobody else would understand.

"In any case, we're not done talking," he continued. "I'm afraid you have me at a disadvantage. You know a little about me, but I know nothing about you. When you're not being accosted by gentlemen at parties," I grinned at the joke, "what is it you do with yourself Sophia?"

"I'm a lawyer."

"Oh I'm so sorry," he said, his voice totally deadpan.

I just laughed. In my profession you rarely go more than a week or two without some kind of lawyer joke. It comes with the territory, and you learn not to take it seriously. "I know, right? If you want to turn and run I won't hold it against you."

"I'll keep that in mind. There are a few other lawyers here tonight actually. You didn't happen to come with any of them did you?"

My stomach clenched. There it was; a question I couldn't answer. My gut told me there were no unaccompanied women in the room, so I'd have to have a partner, and while he might not know everyone, I doubted I could bluff my way through it.

"A lady doesn't kiss and tell," I replied, trying my best to look coy. Inside, I was panicking. If he pressed the issue, that would be it. The jig would be up.

For a few seconds I was certain it was over, but eventually he broke into a laugh. "I'm sorry Sophia, I didn't mean to pry. I was just curious if there were any gentlemen lurking nearby who might be preparing to leap in and defend your honour."

I raised my eyebrows. "I didn't realise my honour was under threat."

His eyes seemed to flicker ever so briefly. "Give me a chance. We've only been talking a few minutes."

His directness was both offensive and exciting. I found

myself wondering what it might be like to succumb to his advances. Even now, just sitting and talking, there was something fiercely attractive about him. I knew he'd be mind-blowing in bed. He exuded that sort of dominant authority that sent logic and self-restraint tumbling to the wayside.

Get a grip Sophia. This cannot happen.

"You seem rather sure of yourself," I said, trying my hardest to act unperturbed.

He gave a little laugh. "I prefer to think of myself as optimistic."

In truth, I doubted his confidence was misplaced. I struggled to see many women rejecting him, however blunt he was.

I realised then that I had to get away. The attraction I felt for him was verging on dangerous, and the longer we talked, the more likely it was that I'd do something stupid.

...okay, something *else* stupid.

"Well, unfortunately I'm going to have to leave your hopes dashed this time," I said. "I am actually here with someone, and it's about time I got back to him. I just left to get a refill, and that was ten minutes ago."

He studied me for several seconds. I expected him to look at least a little disappointed, but instead he seemed vaguely amused. "That's a pity," he said eventually. "But perhaps we'll run into one another again?"

"Perhaps." *No fucking way.*

"Excellent. Well, have a good evening Sophia." And with that, he turned and walked off into the crowd.

I blinked a few times and followed his receding form with my eyes, trying to work out what had just happened. It was like someone had climbed inside me and turned my hormones up to eleven. My heart was still thundering in my chest. *Fantastic Sophia. Ten minutes with tall, dark, and charming and you're hyperventilating like a twelve year old at a Justin Bieber concert. What the hell is wrong with you?*

I took a deep breath and downed the rest of my drink in a single large gulp, hoping to jar my mind into action. As attractive as he was, pursuing him was not an option. All my reservations aside, I'd barely escaped our conversation without being exposed, and somehow I doubted he'd be so friendly if he knew the truth.

Besides, there was something almost terrifying about the way my body responded to him. Even now, I couldn't shake the image of those piercing eyes from my mind.

Glancing around, I suddenly became aware of how exposed I was. Nobody else in the room was standing alone. None of the guests had taken notice yet, but some of the staff were giving me strange looks. I knew I should take the opportunity to get the hell out of dodge, but I wasn't quite ready to face the girls just yet. The alcohol, the adrenaline, the lingering arousal; it was a potent cocktail. My mind was reeling. I needed somewhere to regroup.

"Excuse me," I said, to a pretty brunette behind the bar who was busy shaking up a lurid cocktail the colour of toxic waste, "where are the bathrooms?"

She gestured vaguely to the back of the room. "Just over there."

"Great, thanks."

I walked briskly, doing my best not to make eye contact with anyone. The girl's directions hadn't been very clear, but eventually I found an open doorway stashed in the far corner of the room. On the other side lay a corridor that ran for thirty feet and then hooked off to the right. There were no signs of any bathrooms.

I debated doubling back, but I hadn't seen any other likely openings. I figured they were just deeper in. So I began to explore.

Chapter 3

For a moment after rounding the corner, I thought I'd found what I was looking for. The next hallway was lined with doors. But as I drew closer, I saw that rather than 'Gents' or 'Ladies', they were all marked with heavy brass name tags bearing identical logos. Not bathrooms. Personal offices.

My eyes darted back down the passage as I suddenly became aware of where I was. Sneaking into a party was one thing, but prowling through corporate property was quite another. It was a strange location to put offices, but I didn't have time to puzzle it out. If caught, I'd be in serious trouble.

I turned to go, but it was too late. Voices began to echo up the corridor from the direction I'd come. My heart leapt up into my throat. I was cut off.

Even as panic set in, my mind began hunting for an escape. Running was out of the question with all that security, and the deeper I went into the building, the more trouble I'd likely be in if found. I could try talking my way out, but I'd already had my share of close calls tonight and my lies wouldn't hold up under any real scrutiny. That left only one choice that I could see.

I dove for the nearest door. The voices were getting louder. They sounded like they were just around the bend. By some miracle, the door wasn't locked. I yanked it open, threw myself inside and pulled it shut as softly as my shaking hands would allow. It closed with a quiet but audible click.

I held my breath and pressed my ear against it. The conversation was muted through the thick timber, but it sounded as though the speakers had stopped moving. I could hear them talking — arguing it sounded like — somewhere to my left.

I exhaled slowly, taking the moment's respite to study my hiding place. Having seen the bar outside, the office was no surprise. Opulent, masculine, and sophisticated. The floor was polished wood, the furniture sparse but beautiful, and all of it looked almost too old for anyone to actually risk using. Everything the owner could want was within reach, from a well-stocked bar to an en-suite to a small built-in wardrobe filled with pressed suits. I could probably have lived there and been relatively comfortable.

After a minute had passed, the voices still hadn't moved. Maybe they'd gone into one of the other offices. With any luck that would be as close as they came. All I had to do was wait them out.

Seemingly in no immediate danger, I slipped off my shoes and moved to explore the room a little. It was unlikely they'd hear my footsteps, but I wasn't taking any chances.

There was a laptop open on the desk with a password prompt on the screen. The user name read 'S.Lock'. *Well Mr Lock, your office is a hell of a lot neater than mine.*

Next to the computer was a single stack of papers. Unable to stop myself, I thumbed through the top couple of sheets. At first, I thought it might have been some kind of joke, because the front page was stamped 'Top Secret' in bright red ink, but as I skimmed through it, I began to get the sense that there might be more to it. If it was a hoax, it was an incredibly detailed one. It seemed to be some kind of internal US government document. The content was largely alien to me — most of it had to do with oil in the Middle East — but as I ran my eyes over it, I got the distinct sense that it was a dangerous thing to be reading.

I was so focused on those pages that I nearly missed the sound of voices echoing up the hallway once more. By the time I noticed, they were right outside the door.

Oh Jesus!

Reacting purely on instinct, I scooped up my shoes and bolted for the nearest hiding spot; the cupboard. It was close, but I narrowly made it. The latch clicked shut behind me moments before I heard the rattle of a handle being turned. My pulse was hammering in my ears.

"—don't care what you do, I just need you to take care of it. Losing those panels will put us months behind schedule."

My stomach sank even lower. I knew that elegant voice. S.Lock. I hadn't just stumbled through any door. This was Sebastian's office.

Shit shit shit.

How unlucky could I get?

I crouched down, putting my eyes level with a row of slats towards the bottom of the door, and the room sprung into view. Sebastian was pacing behind the desk, talking to another man who was leaning against the door frame.

"I'll do what I can, but it's not like they left a nice polite note or anything," said the visitor. "It's going to take a little time."

"Well, not getting them back is not an option."

The other man raised his hands defensively. "Okay, okay. I'll get some people on it."

"Good. And send Hannah in on your way out would you?"

"Sure."

He closed the door, leaving Sebastian staring contemplatively into the air. After about thirty seconds, there was a knock, and the girl from before peeked her head in. "You wanted to see me, sir."

"Hannah. Yes, come in."

She walked slowly into the room, a penitent look on her face.

"Well, do you have anything to say for yourself?" he asked.

"I'm sorry, sir."

"Sorry for what?" His voice was hard and unforgiving.

"I'm sorry that I interrupted you."

"We've worked on this before," he said, starting to pace once more. "It's not your position to decide who I can and can't talk to. That's not part of our deal."

She nodded quickly. "I know, sir. I'm sorry."

I shifted uncomfortably. I didn't understand. Hannah was a grown woman, and Sebastian's employee, but she was being chastised as though she was a child.

"Unfortunately Hannah, sorry isn't good enough. You know the rules. What do we do with girls that misbehave?"

Hannah stared at him, wide-eyed, clearly dreading answering the question. "We punish them," she squeaked eventually.

"Indeed."

Oh my god. No wonder their relationship had seemed strange. I wasn't so naive as to not be familiar with BDSM, but I'd always thought of it as a niche fetish, something relegated to kinky underground sex clubs and the odd upper middle class basement. Truthfully, the whole idea seemed vaguely ridiculous. What kind of self-respecting woman gave up control of herself to her partner? It defied all logic. But crouched in that cupboard, watching Sebastian display such visceral control, I felt a small tingle of excitement. Part of me wanted to know what happened next.

He gazed at Hannah for several seconds. "I think it will be the black paddle today." She whimpered. "Go on now," he continued, "you know what to do."

I watched, mesmerised, as Hannah headed slowly over to the wall, opened up a small and rather cleverly hidden cupboard, and withdrew a long leather paddle. My mouth went dry at the sight of it. It was a scary looking implement about two feet long, and coated length to tip in rough, black leather. It seemed out of place given the class and sophistication of our surroundings.

I suppressed a morbid laugh as Sebastian's comment from before finally clicked. *"We'll find time for a paddle later."*

With the object in hand, Hannah hesitated momentarily.

"Bring it to me," said Sebastian, who had removed his jacket and began to roll up his sleeves. His arms were long and lean, but layered with taut ropes of muscle, like those of a professional tennis player.

Hannah sucked in a deep breath. For a second, I thought she was going to resist, but after steeling herself, she marched dutifully back across the room and placed the paddle in Sebastian's fingers. He swished it through the air a few times, testing the weight of it. "Perfect. Now, present yourself for me."

Trembling, she bent over the side of the desk. I was shocked that she was being so compliant, but on some level, I understood. The authority radiating from Sebastian now was almost palpable; a singular force of relentless will. Everything about him spoke of man in utter control; from the weight of his voice to the certainty in his eyes to the measured purposefulness of his movements. There was no doubt in his mind that Hannah would give him what he wanted, and as much as I hated to admit it, I found that determination incredibly arousing.

Sebastian growled in appreciation as he peeled Hannah's skirt back, exposing her naked ass to the air. "It frustrates me that we have to keep doing this," he said, reaching out to cup one cheek, "but I suppose it does have its advantages."

Hannah shifted, drawing in sharp little breaths while he caressed her roughly. As I watched, I found myself wondering what his touch would feel like on my body. His hands looked so strong, and there was something so possessive about the way he stroked her.

"Are you ready for your punishment?" Sebastian asked.

"Yes sir."

"Good."

I wasn't sure what to expect next. It seemed like there should be some kind of preamble, but instead, Sebastian simply whipped the paddle back and brought it crashing down into Hannah's ass.

"One. Thank you, sir," Hannah said through gritted teeth. He spanked again. "Two. Thank you, sir."

God, she even has to thank him. That's one thing you'd never catch me doing.

...or any of this other stuff either.

Jesus Sophia.

Clearly Sebastian was an experienced practitioner. He truly looked in his element now. Every gesture was graceful and precise, and with every stroke, his body flexed and bulged. I hadn't thought it possible, but somehow the situation made him look even more attractive. I felt the unmistakable throb of desire pulsing between my legs.

A glance at Hannah told me I wasn't the only one enjoying myself. Sebastian was so powerful, and every blow looked more excruciating than the last, but as he settled into his rhythm, the shock on her face gradually melted away, replaced with something I could only describe as a kind of pained ecstasy.

Watching her take pleasure in being punished was confronting, but also strangely exciting. The dynamic between them was so raw and so intense that I could practically taste it in the air. I shifted uncomfortably, desperately willing my arousal away, but all I succeeded in doing was knocking a suit off the bar behind me. I caught it with an outstretched hand, but the damage had already been done. In an instant the closet door was flung open and I was once again pinned in place by that penetrating gaze.

Sebastian stared at me for several seconds. I saw him reacting a hundred different ways in my head, but eventually he surprised me by breaking into a laugh. "Well, well, well. Sophia. We did say we might see each other again, but I hadn't expected it to be quite like this." Strangely, he didn't seem surprised, just amused.

I gazed up at him with gaping eyes, blushing furiously. I didn't know what I could possibly say. The whole situation had gotten way out of hand. I briefly debated trying to talk my way out, but judging by the twinkle in his eye, the time for that had passed.

So I did the only thing I could think of.

I ran.

I leapt out of the cupboard and bolted for the hallway. He probably could have stopped me if he'd wanted — the gap between his leg and the cupboard door wasn't very large — but he didn't move, he just watched me, a curious smile on his face.

Before I knew it, I was in the corridor, and then the main room. The guests all stared as I tore across the wooden floor, but I ignored them. All I cared about was getting somewhere safe. Every part of me felt frayed, confused, agitated.

At some point, it occurred to me that I'd left my shoes behind. *Just like Cinderella,* I thought. *Although I'm not sure if the story traditionally contains quite so much masochism.*

For some reason, that thought struck me as perversely funny. I began to laugh as I ran. By the time I broke through into the bar's main room, I was cackling like a street corner drunk.

I was certain someone would be chasing me, but there were no signs of pursuit. Even the door guard was mysteriously absent.

"Come on," I panted to my gaping friends as I charged over to them, "we've gotta bail."

"Wha—"

"Now!"

They didn't argue further.

Thirty seconds later we were half way up the street, giggling with the adrenaline of a successful escape. They didn't even know what we were running from, but the fact that we were running was enough.

"So," Louisa said, when we finally began slowing down, "what the hell was that? What happened back there?"

"You're not going to believe me."

"Try us," Ruth said, looking at me with a mixture of disbelief and curiosity.

And so I told my tale. I described everything as best I could, the grand room, meeting Sebastian, my accidental corporate espionage. The only thing I omitted was the spanking. Something about it made me feel decidedly uncomfortable.

"That's crazy," Louisa said, when I was done.

Ruth shook her head. "You see? She sneaks in there, and five minutes later she's bagged a mysterious millionaire. I told you we should have followed her!"

"I'd hardly use the word 'bagged'," I replied. "Last I checked, trespassing and breaking and entering weren't exactly the keys to a man's heart, although perhaps I'm just out of touch."

Ruth laughed. "You're such a glass half empty kind of girl."

"Hey, I'm just glad he didn't call the cops." I turned to Louisa. "Lou, next time I try to do something like that, do a better job of talking me out of it, would you?"

"I'll do my best," she replied with a grin.

It was just a few hours shy of sunrise at that point, and so we went our separate ways. I caught a cab home and collapsed into bed without even bothering to change. I was exhausted and expected to fall asleep quickly, but my mind was still restless. Whenever I closed my eyes, I saw Sebastian staring down at me with that breathtaking gaze. Whatever his bedroom predilections, there was something undeniably alluring about him. I couldn't remember the last man that had set my heart racing so easily.

Chapter 4

The following morning was far from pleasant. I woke feeling like I'd loaned my head to a marching band. I debated simply rolling over and going back to sleep, but there was too much to do at the office. "You can sleep when you're dead," was a popular catch phrase amongst the Partners, and as much as they grinned when they said it, you knew they were being perfectly serious. Don't get me wrong, Little Bell wasn't any worse than any other big firm — technically it was named Bell & Little, but nobody called it that, no matter how many stern memos went out — it was just the norm in big law to bleed your employees for every drop you could.

A long shower, a coffee, and the world's greasiest ham and cheese croissant later, I was sitting in the back of a cab feeling marginally more human. But apparently I still didn't look it. As I exited the lift on my floor of the building, I ran into my friend Elle. She took one look at me and burst out laughing. "Big night hey Soph?"

I glanced down at myself and grimaced. "That obvious hey?"

Elle nodded. "You look a little haggard, yeah."

There's a funny camaraderie within law firms. Because we all work such long hours, we naturally become friendly. A lot of lawyers have no social lives outside of work. But it's always felt a little fake to me. Behind the niceties, there's as much backstabbing and petty bullying as in any school playground. With most of my colleagues, I kept my distance, but Elle was the exception. Unlike almost everybody else, she didn't buy into all the office bullshit, which meant we'd quickly become friends.

"What can I say? The girls are a bad influence."

Elle flashed an indulgent grin. We'd been out enough times together that she knew who incited most of the drinking. "Well, I hope you've saved some energy for tonight. Drunk Partners, a huge group of self-important corporate types; it's practically your perfect evening."

Shit. I'd completely forgotten about that. A few times a year, our company threw a party for all of its long standing clients. A kind of thank-you-please-keep-giving-us-buckets-of-money type deal. It seemed to work because our profits just kept climbing, but I hated those evenings. There was only so much corporate asskissery I could stomach. Unfortunately, we were all expected to be there if we could make it. We didn't actually do anything; the puppet masters just liked showing us off. A flexing of the company's considerable legal muscle. I usually made it tolerable by taking abundant advantage of the open bar, but with the memory of the morning's hangover still fresh in my mind, I wasn't sure I'd even be doing that.

"I kind of wish you hadn't reminded me. I could have slept through it and not felt guilty."

Elle chuckled again. "Oh come on, it won't be that bad. Do your bit, brown nose a few CEOs. Who knows, you might impress someone."

"And you'll be doing the same?"

"Hell no. I'll be drinking in a corner."

"That sounds like a better plan," I agreed.

33

A tiny smile appeared on her face. "So did you hear?"

"About what?"

"The Wrights case is a go."

My eyes widened. "No way. That's awesome!"

"I know right? It's going to be kind of novel actually doing something worthwhile, instead of just helping companies shit on one another day after day."

I nodded. It was exactly the kind of case I'd always wanted to work on. A David and Goliath class action suit between a group of Average Joes and a pharmaceutical giant. It felt like our own little Erin Brockovich moment.

The situation was horrible. Wrights had hidden the side effects of one of their antidepressants from the general public. The drugs worked fine on most people, with one notable exception. Pregnant women. It was only after several years that someone began joining the dots between the drug in question and the spate of juvenile health problems that followed. Now there were thousands of affected children out there, suffering everything from physical abnormalities to heart conditions. More than a few had died from their complications. It made me angry just thinking about it.

Beyond the chance to do something good, the case was also great publicity for the company, which meant it had the attention of the suits upstairs. There had never been a better opportunity to prove myself.

"Anyway, I have to run these to Freidburg," Elle said, gesturing to the pages in her hand, "but I'll catch you later, okay? Don't even think about sneaking home. I'm not sure I can sit through this one alone."

I raised my hands in defeat. "Okay, okay."

The day chugged along at an agonising crawl. Law isn't nearly as glamorous as it appears on television. Behind every dramatic hour in court there are hundreds of hours of paper-work.

At six o'clock, an office wide email went out calling everyone to the upstairs boardroom. We always hosted our gatherings in-house. For a company the size of Little Bell, appearances were everything, and we'd spent a lot of money making sure we could entertain with the best of them. With the tables cleared away, the band in place, and the bar and canapés laid out, the whole place had the classy but vaguely sterile feel of an expensive wedding reception.

Most of my colleagues were already there when I arrived. Seeing everyone standing together in one place really emphasised the gender imbalance in the company. There were jackets and ties as far as the eye could see. We had a few women on every floor, and a couple had even made it to the lofty ranks of Partner, but the firm was still very much entrenched in the old way of doing things.

Despite my earlier reservations, I decided I couldn't get through the evening without a least one drink, so I snagged a glass of champagne on its way past and then set out in search of a friendly face.

"You made it!" Elle said, as I found her at the other end of the bar. She was chatting to one of the new junior associates, a friendly young guy named Miles.

"You sound surprised," I replied.

"Well, this morning you did look a little like you might keel over at your desk."

"What, and miss all this?" I asked, gesturing dramatically to the room.

"It does have a certain... unique charm," Miles said, wearing a bemused smile.

"First time?" I asked.

He nodded.

"You're working under Alan right?"

He nodded again.

Elle and I shared an eye roll. "Has he taken you to run the executive gauntlet yet?" she asked

"I don't think so," he replied.

"Well, don't worry, he will," I said. "He likes to start grooming his flock early."

He gave a nervous little laugh. "I'm not sure I like the idea of being groomed."

"Me either," I replied. "Certainly helps if you want an actual career though."

His brow furrowed. "What do you mean by that?"

I gazed at him for several seconds, my tongue poised on my lips, before shaking my head. I didn't have the energy for a rant right now. Besides, he'd see soon enough. "Never mind. Forget I said anything."

"No, hang on," he persisted, "you can't make a comment like that and then just let it go."

Elle had been watching the exchange with a mixture of amusement and resignation. She understood. She was in the same boat as me. "What she means is, this place is very cliquey. You get in with the right people early, you're set."

He filled in the obvious blank. "And if you don't?"

Elle shot me a glance and raised her eyebrows.

I sighed. "Then expect to be shovelling shit for quite a few years."

He chewed the inside of his cheek thoughtfully. "How long have you two been here?"

"Six years for me, five for Elle," I replied.

"And you're both still juniors?" he asked.

I nodded.

"Fuck. I take it that's not normal?"

I shrugged. "Depends on your definition of normal. If

you don't kiss the right asses then yeah, that's pretty much the way it goes."

"Speaking of ass kissing, have you met the office's resident brown nosing queen yet, Miles?" Elle asked, nodding to the woman who was approaching us from across the room.

"Can't say that I've had the pleasure," he replied.

I grimaced. "Well it looks like you're about to get your chance."

There was nobody in the office I disliked more than Jennifer Smart. The two of us had started at Little Bell around the same time, and from day one, we'd seemed destined to be rivals. Everything about her rubbed me the wrong way, and although she was as sweet as honey to my face, I knew the feeling was mutual. I'd assumed my eighty hour weeks and pristine work would trump her grovelling, but apparently I'd been mistaken. Two years ago she'd made Senior Associate, while I was still stuck shuffling paper. It was a victory she savoured to this day.

"Sophia!" she said, flashing me a perfect beauty pageant smile. She had her fake nice act down to a fine art, but truth be told, I still didn't understand why so many people were fooled. There was something inherently unpleasant behind those angular features, a callousness that no amount of phony warmth could hide.

"I was wondering if you'd be here," she continued. "I know you don't much care for these little gatherings."

"Wouldn't miss it for the world, Jennifer," I replied, forcing myself to sound vaguely polite.

"Well good. It's good to keep in touch with our clients, don't you think? Speaking of which," she nodded at the older gentleman standing next to her, "this is Mr Chardy. He's the head of development at Marvin Lemac. We've been handling their fraud case."

37

I gritted my teeth. She had the most frustrating habit of making out that nobody else knew what was going on around the office except her. "I know who you are," I said to him, holding out my hand. "I'm Sophia Pearce. It's a pleasure to meet you."

"Likewise."

The others introduced themselves.

"Sophia, Elle, and Miles here are all part of our junior associate team," Jennifer continued. "I know when you meet with us it might seem like it's just me or Alan handling your case, but we really couldn't do what we do without these guys. They're the ones doing all the grunt work."

"Well you've done an excellent job so far," Chardy said.

I nodded in thanks, not trusting myself to speak. Back-handed compliments were Jennifer's speciality.

She glanced around the room. "Well anyway, it's been lovely chatting to you, but I want to introduce Joseph here to a few more people. You know how it is; so many Partners, so little time. Have a good night."

Taking his arm she led him off into the crowd.

"Well, she didn't seem that bad," Miles said, when she was out of earshot.

"Are you kidding?" Elle replied. "That smile was so sweet I think I threw up a little in my mouth."

"Have either of you actually done any work on the Marvin Lemac case?" I asked. They both shook their heads. "Exactly. She didn't need to introduce him at all. It was just another excuse to gloat." I threw back the rest of my champagne in a single long sip. "Fucking 'grunt work' indeed. I could strangle that bitch."

"It sounded like a compliment to me," Miles said quietly.

Elle and I looked at one another before bursting out laughing. "You have a lot to learn about this place," I told him. "Anyway, after that, I think I could use another drink. Back in a sec."

I could see my plans for a dry night evaporating before my eyes, but if that meeting was a sign of things to come, I'd need all the help I could get. Little did I know things were about to get even worse.

"What can I get you?" said the guy behind the bar.

And for the second time in as many days, someone answered for me. "She'll have a Cosmo. And get me another beer."

I rolled my eyes. "Actually, I'll have a glass of Shiraz," I said, turning to frown at my new companion. Taylor had started on my floor a year earlier, and since day one, he'd been trying to lure me into bed. I might have taken it as a compliment, if he hadn't done the same thing to every woman in the office. Sadly, many of them fell for it.

Objectively, I guess he was good looking, in that blonde, bulky, frat boy kind of way, but he was such a gigantic ass that I found it impossible to see anything else. His daddy was some big hedge fund type who was friends with everybody, so Taylor spent his entire life coasting around on his enormous sense of entitlement. I think it annoyed him that I was so resistant to his 'charms', although he'd never say it.

"If you're going to order for a girl, at least pay attention to what she's drinking, genius."

He gave a little laugh. "Hey, I was just trying to be friendly. Do you always bite guys' heads off when they try to buy you drinks?"

"This is the company bar, so you're not buying me anything."

He flashed a smile that he probably thought was seductive. "Not here I'm not."

I exhaled sharply. "Not anywhere."

"Come on Sophia, at least hear me out. It's no secret you hate these things, so what say you and I get out of here? My dad owns this sweet little wine bar just a block from my apartment. We could drink whatever we want, on the house. No Cosmos there, I promise."

I had to give him points for persistence, but at that moment I really just wished he'd disappear.

I looked him straight in the eyes and grazed my teeth slowly across my bottom lip in that way that guys seem to love. "Close to your apartment, hey?"

His face lit up. "That's right."

"What about your dad? Does he live nearby too?"

He blinked several times in confusion. "My dad?"

"Yeah. I mean if we're drinking on the house, that would mean it's really him buying me drinks. It'd feel kind of rude going home with someone else after that."

His expression crumbled, and I gave myself a little internal high five.

"Well, we could go somewhere else if you like..." he said lamely.

And then someone else spoke from behind me. "I don't think she's going anywhere with you." My heart turned a cartwheel in my chest.

Even before I looked, I recognised the voice; low and strong and smooth as caramel. For a moment I was overcome by a powerful sense of deja vu, but it passed as the reality of the situation came crashing into me.

"Hello Sophia," Sebastian said, sliding in next to me. "It's lovely to see you again."

I stared at him with wide eyes, my tongue frozen in shock. He was the last person in the world I'd ever expected to see again. But there he was in front of me, smiling like he hadn't caught me huddled in his office cupboard just a day earlier.

Taylor wasn't so easily rattled. He rocked back on his heels, an incredulous smile blooming on his face. "Hey buddy, we're having a conversation here."

Sebastian's eyes flicked to him. There was no anger there. If anything, he looked vaguely amused. "No, you're harassing a girl who quite clearly wants to be left alone."

Taylor bristled. "And I suppose she'd rather be talking to you?"

"She'd rather be doing a lot of things."

It was my turn to bristle, but nobody was paying any attention to me anymore. It was like I'd disappeared. They loomed up from either side of me, staring at one another as though they could make their adversary's head explode through sheer force of will. It was almost comical really, but laughter was about as far out of reach for me as humanely possible at that moment.

"Is that right?" Taylor asked, his jaw tightening. "And just who might you be, friend?" He gave that last word a sharp accent.

"Just a man who would like a word with Sophia, if you don't mind." In spite of the phrasing, there was no question in his voice.

Taylor continued to stare. Pissing contests like this weren't exactly uncommon around the office. Give a bunch of overachieving jocks huge salaries and inflated senses of self-worth, and you're just asking for testosterone to fly. When push came to shove, Taylor usually came out on top, but this time I could tell he was losing. There was something so utterly indomitable about Sebastian. From the easy confidence of his smile to the raw intensity of his gaze and the dangerous grace of his movements, he was the epitome of a man who knew he'd get what he wanted. Taylor may have been his physical equal, but whatever primal hormonal reaction decided the

41

outcome of those sorts of engagements was telling him to head for the hills.

After a few seconds, he looked away. "Fine," he spat, snatching up his beer. "I'll see you around, Sophia." Turning, he stalked off into the crowd.

I shook my head slowly. "What the fuck was that?" I spluttered, finally finding my voice.

"That was me saving you from an unpleasant conversation." Sebastian didn't look even slightly embarrassed.

"Saving me? I was talking to a colleague! What if I was enjoying myself?"

He gave a little laugh. "What, with that guy?"

I shook my head slowly, trying to gather my thoughts. His approach was nothing short of infuriating, but there were more important things to focus on.

"Whatever. That's beside the point. What the hell are you doing here, Sebastian?"

"I wanted to see you again," he said, like it was the most natural thing in the world.

I had no idea how to respond. As confusing as it all was, part of me was happy to see him too. Just being near him again set something thrumming inside me. He looked every bit as gorgeous as he had the previous night. He'd traded his charcoal three-piece for a simple navy business suit, but it still did little to disguise the exquisite musculature beneath. His hair tumbled in long curls around his perfectly hewn face, framing a smile that hit me like a punch to the chest.

"Surely there are easier ways to go about that. Like, maybe, a phone call?" I said.

He laughed. "And would you have agreed to see me if I'd just rung?"

"I guess not," I said slowly. "But I don't appreciate being taken by surprise, either. How did you even manage to find me? And how did you get in here? This is my office!"

"It wasn't as difficult as you may think. There are only so many striking young lawyers named Sophia in Sydney." He glanced around. "As for how I got in, well Laurence Bell is actually an old acquaintance of my company. Once I knew where you worked, it was easy enough to organise an invitation."

He knew Mr Bell? That was odd. Our boss was a notorious recluse. Yeah, his name was on the sign outside, but he rarely even came into the office anymore. He was like the good china that only got brought out for special occasions.

Sebastian continued to stare, those magnificent eyes once again boring deep inside me. It made me uncomfortable. Sure, he was hot, and we'd gotten along well, but the whole situation had my hairs standing on end. Judging by last night, there was no shortage of women in his life. He had no reason to track me down. No reason, unless he was angry about having his privacy invaded.

"Well, I don't think this is appropriate," I said, shaking my gaze free.

"You mean after the way we left things last night?"

My cheeks heated. "Look, about that, I can explain..."

"About what? Breaking into my office? Or sneaking into our gathering?" He smiled at my expression. "That's right, I know. In fact I knew the whole time. You're not the only one who can act, Sophia."

I closed my eyes briefly and drew a slow breath. "So why talk to me? Why not just have me thrown out?"

"Does a man need an excuse to chat to a beautiful girl now?"

I rolled my eyes. "Yeah, because pretty girls were in short supply last night."

He grinned, and I felt myself melt just a little more. "Well to be honest, security was ready to escort you out the moment you walked in. We always have more than one set of eyes on that door. But I stopped them."

"Why?"

He shrugged. "I was curious. I wanted to know what kind of girl you were. Plenty of people have tried talking their way through that doorway over the years, but very few actually succeed." His expression remained mild as he spoke. He certainly didn't seem angry, but it was hard to tell what lay behind that charming exterior.

"Well, thank you for not making a scene. I'm sorry I intruded. I was just messing around and it got out of hand. I never meant to go into your office at all."

"You could make it up to me by coming home with me tonight."

I did a double take, certain I must have misheard him. In light of everything that had happened, the request seemed completely absurd.

"Are you joking?"

"Why would I be joking?"

"Oh, I don't know, because the last time you saw me I was huddled in your office cupboard, watching you smack your secretary like a child?"

"You didn't enjoy the show?" he asked, not the least bit ashamed.

I snorted. "It was a little Dita Von Tease for my tastes."

That only widened his smile. "Is that so? People are always afraid of what they don't understand. Don't write it off so easily. You might be surprised by what you'd enjoy." The certainty in his voice was unsettling. It sounded less like a suggestion and more like a promise. I shuffled awkwardly on my feet, memories of last night's strange excitement echoing through my mind. I still didn't know why I'd reacted like that.

This is what happens when you let your dry spells last too long. Even a spanking starts to seem appealing. You need to get laid, girl.

"Well sorry to disappoint you, but that's not my style," I said, doing my best to keep my voice level, "so I'm sure my vanilla sensibilities will be incredibly boring for you."

He reached out and brushed my neck lightly, raking his eyes over my body. "I doubt I could ever find *this* boring, regardless of what we're doing."

I swallowed loudly. My mouth suddenly felt like it had been baking in the sun for hours. As much as I hated to admit it, his overt sexuality was a huge turn on. There was nothing sleazy about it. He was just a man who was utterly comfortable with himself and his desires. Once again, I found myself imaging what it might be like to give myself to him. There was no other way to describe it. With other men, I might have said 'sleep with' or 'fuck' or one of the hundred other euphemisms that springs to mind at such times, but with Sebastian, I got the sense none of those were quite right. Even with nothing kinky involved, sex with him would not merely be physical, it would be an act of sheer possession and power.

Focus, Sophia. Think unsexy thoughts. Paperwork. Schindler's List. Ernest in a skirt.

Urgh, too far.

"What makes you even sure I *want* to sleep with you?" I said, purposefully pulling away from him. I swear it was like he had his own personal gravity.

Annoyingly, this just made him laugh. "Is that really how you want to play this?"

"I'm not playing."

"Well neither am I. You can pretend if you want, but it doesn't change a thing." He leaned in close, as though whispering a secret. That intoxicating scent hit my nose once more, sending my hormones into overdrive. "Your body says more than any words ever could."

A shiver rolled through me, coming to rest firmly in the centre of my chest. I hated how easily he could read me. It made me feel strangely helpless. How do you fend off a man who already seems to know your secrets?

"You're right, my body is saying a lot of things," I said. "Like leave me the hell alone! I've been with men like you before, Sebastian. Hell, I work with them every day. Even if I was attracted to you, I wouldn't be interested in being another notch on the bed post."

"What makes you think that's all you'd be?"

I scoffed. "Because we just met yesterday — in rather extenuating circumstances, I might add — and now you're asking me to go to bed with you?"

He shrugged like it was par for the course. "I prefer to be up front in my relationships. That way there's no mixed messages. No one gets hurt."

"Well, that's very noble of you, but I get the impression we don't want the same things."

"And what is it you want, Sophia?"

"Well, call me old fashioned, but something more than, 'hey, want to fuck?' would be a good start."

"I didn't pick you for a flowers and chocolates kind of girl."

"I'm not. I'm too busy for that crap. Casual suits me just fine. But there's a difference between casual and meaningless."

"Good, then we're on the same page. Look, you're right, I'm not the sort of guy that dates. I don't have the time or the inclination to be tied down, and I make no apologies for that. But that doesn't automatically make me some asshole who just uses women and then throws them away. If there's no spark, I'm not interested. And this right here, this has got me

46

very interested."

I laughed. "Ah, the playa with a heart of gold. How touching. But unfortunately, I'm not good at sharing. I have this weird thing about wanting the men I sleep with to only be sleeping with me."

He let out a long breath. "Well, I don't usually do exclusivity."

I recoiled in mock surprise. "I'm shocked!"

He studied me for a few seconds, his expression hovering somewhere between frustration and amusement. "This doesn't have to be complicated, Sophia. There are so many things I want to do to that body of yours, and I promise that you'll enjoy every exquisite minute of it. Why do you need anything more than that?"

Something in my lower belly clenched. Despite how crude his approach was, I believed him. And a rather loud voice in the back of my head was begging me to let him have his wish.

But somehow, I rallied one more time. "It's not complicated for me. It's incredibly simple. I'm. Not. Interested! Now if you'll excuse me, I'm going to go back to my friends. I'll extend you the same courtesy you extended me and let you walk yourself out, but if I see you here again, I'm calling security. I don't care who your friends are, if you're harassing an employee, you'll be out of here before you can blink. Goodbye, Sebastian. It's been... interesting." And with much more confidence than I felt inside, I spun and marched away.

I could hardly blame him for the way my body reacted to his, but it was still immensely satisfying to storm off like that. *That'll teach him to get into my head. Bastard.*

I expected maybe a parting shot, but no words followed me. I resisted the urge to turn and look back. I was proud of myself for not caving to him, although there were very specific parts of me that were emphatically venting their disappointment. I suspected I'd be delving into my underwear drawer later for a little relief.

"Jesus Christ," Elle said, as I returned. Miles was nowhere to be seen, but she was peering over my shoulder with an awestruck gaze, her lips hanging slightly open. *At least it's not just me.*

"Who the hell was that?" she asked.

I shrugged. "I'm not sure actually. Just some guy."

"Seriously? That's like calling Ryan Gosling 'just some guy'!"

I shrugged again, trying to feign disinterest. The sooner we stopped talking about him, the better.

"Well, whoever he was, he looked hella into you," she continued.

"You think?" I asked.

She stared at me like I'd gone mad. "He was practically eye fucking you from the moment you guys started talking. How could you not notice that? I even bet Miles ten bucks he'd get your number."

I winced. "Sorry, no dice."

She shook her head slowly. "Fuck. Well, I guess that means he's still fair game, then."

I laughed. "If we see him again, he's all yours."

Our conversation turned to other things. Despite my best efforts, I found myself glancing around every so often, checking that Sebastian wasn't still lurking nearby. It seemed like he'd taken my warning seriously, but I got the sense such threats may not really mean much to him. After all, he'd tracked me down and infiltrated my office as easily as walking through his own front door.

The effortlessness with which he'd done that frightened me a little. When he'd shown up, my mind had been reeling

48

too much to really think it through; but now the reality of the situation was becoming apparent. In a way, it was vaguely flattering that he'd gone to such efforts, but it also made me suspicious. Between that and the bizarre events of the previous night, I got the sense that there was more to Sebastian Lock than he was telling me.

Chapter 5

I spent the next two days on autopilot. Soon, we'd be starting work on the Wrights case, but at that point, it was just business as usual. It felt a little like the calm before the storm. There was already a noticeable buzz around the office, like that frenetic pre-Christmas energy that fills the air as December rolls around. I was excited, but also a little intimidated. We had those people's futures in our hands. Winning wouldn't magically fix the damage, but it would mean hospital bills paid, carers hired, and a huge quality of life improvement for all those affected.

Even without Wrights, we were busy. I usually did my best to at least get out of the office for lunch — there was only so much monochrome decor and recycled air I could take in one day — but my workload meant I just didn't have the time.

So on Saturday, when my boss called asking me to go and meet a new prospective client, I jumped at the chance. I normally hated those schmoozing business lunches, but anything that dragged me away from my screen was a win at that moment.

The meet was at an upmarket steak restaurant in Martin Place named Cuts. It was one of those places that looked like it'd been pulled straight out of the fifties. Dimly lit and dominated by leather and sandstone, it gave off the impression of being expressly made to host boozy lunchtime business rendezvous. I half expected to find the cast of Mad Men hunched in one corner, smoothly wooing prospective clients and chortling over their scotch. I'd been told that the sophisticated aesthetic wasn't just a bluff. The steaks were apparently some of the best in town, although in all honesty, one cut of meat was much the same as any other to me.

I arrived a little early. The restaurant was quiet. There were just a handful of groups dining inside and a lone guy sitting at the bar. I made a beeline for the main room, longing to get a glass of red into me before my client arrived. We hadn't met before — all I had was a name; Mr Keys — but it seemed like a good idea to loosen up a little first.

But as I approached, the man at the bar spun to face me. I froze.

"Are you fucking serious?" I said.

"Not much for traditional greetings are you?" Sebastian asked, clearly enjoying having shocked me for a second time.

As usual, a pang of desire rushed through me at the sight of him. I had no idea how I hadn't noticed him immediately. Even in the simple act of sitting still, that masculine poise was unmistakable.

"Not when I'm talking to men who appear to be stalking me," I replied sharply.

He gave a little laugh. "You arrive after me, but I'm the one stalking you?"

He had a point. I shifted uncomfortably. "Well, whatever. I don't have time for your games today, Sebastian. I'm here for a meeting."

His smile grew. "Me too."

It took me a second. "Oh, you didn't?" I said. But the

smugness in his expression confirmed it. "You bastard."

I thought back over the phone call with my boss. It hadn't occurred to me to ask why I was being sent over anyone else. I just assumed it was a random decision. "You asked for me especially?"

"I did."

Mr Keys. Mr Lock. Fuck. I should have seen it coming. "You can't just waste my time like this, Sebastian. I have a job to do."

"And I respect that. I've already paid for an hour of your time, so we're not wasting anything."

My eyes widened. "You paid that ridiculous fee just to get me down here?"

He nodded.

"Well... fuck." I wish I could say I was surprised, but despite the way we'd left things the other night, I'd had a hunch he wasn't done. He struck me as the sort of man who wasn't used to losing. I guess now I had some idea just how far he was willing to go.

I didn't know what to do. Being near him was dangerous. Even my frustration at his tenacity couldn't blunt the attraction I felt for him. My chest tightened as my eyes roamed involuntarily over the hardness of his body. One elegant hand was resting on the bar, tapping out a slow rhythm against the wood, as if serenading me with a piano ballad. Even his fucking fingers were gorgeous. All I could think about was having them playing across my skin instead.

"Give me ten minutes, Sophia," he said. "After that, I promise I'll leave you alone, if you want."

It seemed like I didn't have much choice. He clearly wasn't giving up without a fight. If I didn't hear him out, he'd be back. Perhaps it was better to end things properly, once and for all.

"Fine. Ten minutes."

He nodded in thanks and led me inside.

"Drink?" he asked, as we slid into our booth.

I shook my head. "I think I'd rather keep my wits about me for now."

I was rewarded with a grin. "Fair enough." He gestured to the waiter to stay put for now.

"I don't really know what else there is to say," I said. "I've told you, we don't want the same things. If you think you can change my mind with tricks and perseverance you've got another thing coming."

"Ah, but what if I have a new proposal?"

I couldn't help but laugh. Everything was like a business deal to him. Approach from different angles until you find one that works.

"Go on then," I said, rolling my eyes. "Make your pitch. But remember, the clock is ticking."

"Dinner."

"Dinner? As in, the two of us?"

He nodded.

"That sounds dangerously close to a date," I replied. "Wouldn't that be breaking the rules?"

He smiled ruefully. "Maybe, but I don't believe you've given me much choice."

"Of course I have. You could just leave me alone instead."

"I don't consider that an option at all."

There was an intensity to those words that was almost frightening. I had no idea how to deal with that. "Well, a meal together is all well and good," I said slowly, "but it doesn't change the fact that I'm not interested in joining your little harem."

As usual, the more caustic my tongue grew, the more it seemed to entertain him. "I get the impression you think I'm more debauched than I really am, Sophia. Just because I like to keep my options open doesn't mean I automatically hit on anything in a skirt."

"Just the skirts you work with then?" I asked.

"Actually, that's the other thing I was going to mention. Hannah is no longer in the picture."

I rocked back in my seat. "What happened?"

"I ended it. To be honest that relationship was a mistake to begin with. I've always made an effort never to mix business and pleasure, but Hannah was rather... eager. In any case, shortly after you left on Tuesday, she blew up at me. It was the last straw. It had gotten too messy."

He made it sound like it had been coming for a while, but the fact that I'd been the catalyst made me feel a little guilty.

I licked my lips. "And there are no other girls?"

"Nope. If you agree, it will be just you and me."

Those words had a lovely ring to them.

"So why not just tell me that the other night at my office?" I asked.

His expression slipped a little. "I was hoping it wouldn't be necessary. Like I said, I'm not entirely comfortable with exclusivity. I find it often leads to people getting too attached too quickly. But I'm willing to make an exception in this case, as long as we understand each other."

I really wanted to believe him. A light, casual, but monogamous relationship was exactly the sort of thing I needed, and he'd gone to such great lengths that it seemed unlikely he was looking to screw me over. But I was still wary. I'd been fooled before by men like him. For some of them, the challenge was even more fun than the victory itself. This could all just be part of the game.

And even if he was being honest, how long would his promises last? How long would a man with his pick of the litter be content to stay in one place?

"Why are you going to all this effort, Sebastian?" I asked, no longer able to disguise the conflict in my voice. "Surely you can get what you need elsewhere."

He smiled a secretive little smile and shook his head slowly. "You don't give yourself enough credit, Sophia. You were the most beautiful girl in the room that first night we met. I bet there are a lot of men out there who would go to great lengths for an evening with you, if only you'd give them the chance."

I blushed and looked away. I didn't think of myself as someone who was easily swayed by flattery, but I had to admit, I loved hearing the desire in Sebastian's voice when he spoke like that. It made me feel sexier than I had in a long time.

"Come on, one meal," he continued. "No strings attached. If you have fun, we'll take it from there, if not, no problem. I'll drop you home and wish you good night and never bother you again."

I could feel my resolve weakening. He was just so gorgeous, and he didn't seem to want to take no for an answer. What was the worst that could happen? It wasn't like I was committing to anything beyond a meal and a chat. I could bail at any time if I felt uneasy.

I closed my eyes and sucked in a deep breath. "Okay fine. One meal. But I'm not promising anything else."

"I'll be a perfect gentleman, I promise," he said, with a laugh. "How's tomorrow night?"

"Fine."

"Okay, I'll pick you up at seven thirty."

"Alright."

He took my hand and kissed it. It was the sort of gesture that's hard to take seriously, but he somehow managed to pull it off. The brush of his lips sent a pulse of warmth shooting between my legs. "Until then, Sophia."

And then he left.

It was only a few minutes later, after I demolished a glass of Shiraz, that I realised I hadn't told him where I lived. But then again, he'd managed to find my office; why would my home address be a problem?

I had no idea how he did the things he did. I'd sat down one hundred percent certain that nothing was going to happen, and yet in just a few short minutes he'd changed my mind. It was like he'd cast a spell on me.

Agreeing to go out with him was probably a mistake. I'd been down that road before with heart breakers like him, and it always ended in tears. I tried to tell myself that nothing was set in stone. Things would only progress as far as I wanted them to. But part of me wasn't sure that was really true. His persistence seemed endless, his magnetism almost irresistible. If he made a move, I wasn't sure I'd be able to stop myself, no matter how much I wanted to.

Chapter 6

The next morning I decided to walk to work. One of the reasons I moved to Newtown is that it's so much fun to stroll through. The people can be a little intense at times, but there's always something interesting going on. Markets, protests, impromptu street performances; it's an eclectic mix of colour and culture. I often go wandering when I need to unwind. There's just something about the vibe that I find relaxing.

After arming myself with caffeine, I slipped onto auto pilot and let my feet guide me the rest of the way. It was mid-October, and the air was just beginning to carry a little of that summer bite. The walk was going to make me late, but at that moment I didn't care. I was just relishing the sunshine.

I'd been trying my best not to think about my impending date, but truth be told, I was nervous. There was something so enigmatic about Sebastian. For the first time in a long time, I had no idea what to expect from a man.

It must have been weighing on me more than I realised, because at some point I veered off my normal route. I didn't even notice, until my eyes fell upon a familiar red shop front, and then it suddenly clicked into place.

Really, Sophia?

My legs had carried me all the way back to the bar from

that first night. In the light of day, it was an even sorrier sight than I remembered. Paint peeled in great ribbons from the walls, and the sign was missing enough letters that I wasn't even sure what it was called. Nobody would ever have guessed the sort of events that were hosted behind that crumbling façade.

The smart thing to do was probably to turn around and keep moving. I'd caused enough trouble there for one week, and I doubted Sebastian would appreciate me prying any more than I already had. But seeing the place again piqued my curiosity. Perhaps it was my chance to learn a little more about the man I'd be spending the evening with.

I wasn't even sure that the bar would be open, but the door fell inward with a creak at my touch. It took my eyes a moment to adjust to the darkness. The room was largely deserted. The only customers were two men, sitting alone in opposite corners, staring glumly into their glasses. They couldn't even muster the energy to look up as I entered.

There was a girl behind the bar who hadn't been there the other night. She blinked in surprise when she saw me. "Can I help you?"

My gaze flicked to the back wall. The door was there, just like I remembered. I let out a long breath. I'm not sure why, but even after seeing Sebastian again, part of me had still been convinced I'd made the whole thing up.

As expected, the door was closed, which suited me just fine. Charging back in for a second time was a sure fire way to get myself caught. What I needed now was a more subtle approach.

"Maybe," I said, approaching the bar. "I was here on Tuesday night for a function with my friend, and I think I left something behind."

The girl looked confused. "Function?"

"Yea, back there," I said, nodding to the back wall.

Her expression grew wary. "Ah." Apparently whatever went on back there was a sore spot for her. "Sorry, I can't help you."

"Please," I said, trying my best to look desperate, "it was a brooch, a gift from my grandmother before she died. It's really important to me. Do you have a lost and found or something?"

Her expression softened. "I'm sorry, I didn't mean to sound rude, but I really can't help. Anything back there stays back there."

"But surely you've got the keys?" I asked.

She shook her head. "Only the owners have access to that door. Apparently we're not 'trustworthy' enough," she said, making air quotes. "To tell you the truth, I've never even been back there."

"But what if someone wants to use it?"

She shook her head. "According to my boss it's not for the public. It's just for them. And they only use it every few months. We're not really meant to ask questions, but it seems kind of weird if you ask me."

"Yeah it does." Why on earth would you have a room that lavish if you're only going to use it a few times a year? And why stash it at the back of a place like this? It made no sense.

The girl leaned in conspiratorially. "You want to hear something even weirder?" I nodded. "We're not even allowed to work when they're using it. That's why I've never been back there. They bring in an entirely new staff, all their own people. Who *does* that?"

I shook my head slowly. "I have no idea."

Her eyes suddenly narrowed. "Hey, shouldn't you know all this already if you were here with them?"

I shrugged. "I'd never been before the other night. Like I

59

said I was just keeping my friend company. I only stayed maybe half an hour."

"Ah, fair enough." A smile bloomed on her face. "So, what was it like back there? I've always wondered."

I felt bad shattering whatever wonderful images she'd conjured in her head, but telling the truth would only make her more inquisitive. She might even get herself into trouble. "Honestly? It was nothing special. A bar, some tables, pretty much like any other corporate function I've been to."

Her shoulders sunk. "Oh. Okay. Well, I'm sorry I couldn't help with your brooch. I could try and ask my boss to speak to the owners if you want..."

"That's okay. I'll see if my friend can talk to them. He's the one who brought me along."

"That might be better, yeah."

"Thanks for your time," I said, turning towards the exit.

"No problem. Bye."

I left the building even more confused than when I'd entered. Everything about the place was slightly off. I only knew one thing for sure; Sebastian and his friends valued their privacy. Perhaps they were simply eccentric in that way that wealthy people sometimes are, but where did those papers on Sebastian's desk fit in?

I knew it was none of my business. Sebastian's secrets were his own, and he didn't owe me any explanations. But nonetheless, I couldn't help but wonder; what on earth had I gotten myself into?

Chapter 7

As the evening drew closer, I began to grow excited. As bizarre as the whole situation was, it had been a long time since I'd been on a date, and never with a man as gorgeous as Sebastian.

It wasn't until I finished showering and went to dress that I realised how unprepared I was for the occasion. I'm not normally the sort of girl who spends half the night getting ready, but the shimmering fabrics and exotic cuts on display at his party had left me feeling strangely self-conscious. Suddenly, nothing I owned seemed even remotely nice enough. I had plenty of jackets, blouses and knee length skirts, and a few cocktail dresses for special occasions, but expensive meals with mysterious millionaires were definitely out of my comfort zone.

Half an hour and more than a handful of failed outfits later, I gave up and headed to the lounge to wait. I was wearing a simple black pencil skirt with a white V-neck top I'd dug from some long forgotten corner of my wardrobe. I assumed it was going to be wildly inappropriate for whatever he had planned, but if he didn't like it, that was his problem. I wasn't about to rush out and go shopping for that perfect something just to please him.

At seven thirty sharp, my doorbell rang.

"I'll be right out," I called.

He was waiting for me on the landing outside, leaning against the wall and gazing out into the street. Despite only seeing him yesterday, somehow I seemed to have forgotten how gorgeous he was. Tonight he wore his dark dinner jacket open at the front, his black shirt unbuttoned at the top to reveal just a hint of the olive skin and cut chest beneath.

Seeing him standing there looking so effortlessly masculine was like having a bucket of water poured over my head. I froze in place, my tongue involuntarily grazing my lips as I drank in the sight of him. The casual look suited him. It made him look more human. A godlike human, but still.

He smiled when he noticed me, those blazing eyes caressing my body like a soft wind, sending a tingle up my spine.

"You look lovely," he said.

I gave a little spin. "Thank you. It's not Prada, but it does the job."

He laughed. "What makes you think I want Prada? You make too many assumptions, Sophia."

"So if I told you this outfit was thirty bucks at Myer, you wouldn't send me back to change?"

"No. I'd say that most girls would kill to look that good for thirty dollars."

"Well if it's value you're looking for, I might be able to get it down to twenty if you give me a few more minutes to change."

He let out a little growl. "I know I said this dinner was strictly no obligations, but if you keep giving me excuses as to why you should remove your clothes, I won't be held responsible for my actions."

I blushed. I hadn't meant it that way, but once again he'd managed to turn an innocent statement into something much hotter.

Looping his arm through mine, he turned and led me down the stairs to the black limousine that was waiting by the kerb.

He nodded to the man who was standing next to the door. "This is my driver, Joe."

"Evening ma'am." Joe was a friendly looking gentleman of about sixty. He had the weathered face of a once sturdy guy who had been through a lot, and as he moved to open the door for us, I noticed that he walked with a bad limp.

"War wound," he said, following my gaze. "Took a shot clean through the knee. Shattered part of the kneecap."

"That's horrible."

He shrugged. "Maybe. I've always thought it rather Lucky myself. A foot higher and I wouldn't be here at all."

I nodded, unsure how to reply.

"Joe's been with me nearly ten years," Sebastian said.

"Has it really been that long, sir? The time has simply flown by." The older man's voice was heavy with sarcasm, but Sebastian merely grinned. Clearly there was more than professional courtesy between the two of them.

"Come on, we'll be late," Sebastian said, guiding me to the open door and ushering me through with a gentle push to the small of my back. Even that somehow felt like an incredibly sensual gesture.

"So where are we headed?" I asked, as the limo pulled out into the street.

"Well, I was lucky enough to get last minute reservations at Quay."

My eyes widened. I wasn't much for fine dining, but I knew enough to know that Quay was as fancy as they came. Now I definitely was under-dressed. "Isn't the waiting list like a month long there?"

He shrugged. "They had a cancellation."

It seemed a little unbelievable, but I didn't push. "So, how you feeling?" I asked instead. "You nervous at all?"

His lips quirked upward. "And why would I be nervous?"

"Well I imagine this is your first date in a while. You know, being the non-dating sort and all."

"Possibly."

"So I thought you might be a little worried. It's okay, it's perfectly natural. Just be yourself, I'm not going to judge."

He looked at me for several seconds then shook his head ruefully. "You're not planning on making this easy are you?"

"I don't know what you mean." I tried to keep my face straight, but a hint of a smile crept through anyway. After feeling constantly off balance with him, it was nice to put him on the back foot for once.

We sat for a few minutes just looking out the window. He'd seemed upbeat initially, but in the silence that followed, that all leeched away. The longer we sat, the darker his expression grew.

"A penny for your thoughts?" I said eventually.

He blinked several times. "Sorry. I didn't mean to be rude. I've just got a lot on my mind."

"Trouble in venture capital paradise?"

He grimaced. "It's not a big deal. One of our projects has just had some setbacks recently. It's frustrating, that's all."

"What kind of project?"

He smiled apologetically. "I'm not really at liberty to talk about it. It's company policy not to discuss our work with other people. We deal with some sensitive stuff from time to time."

Yeah, like US Government documents. I'd been debating whether to raise any of the questions that had been running through my mind. Obviously he had secrets, and that was fine. Casual meant not having to share much of yourself if you didn't want to. But I couldn't resist trying to fish for a little more information.

"Well, whatever you guys do, you throw a mean party, I'll say that much."

"I'm glad you enjoyed yourself. Honestly those don't happen that often. A few times a year when we want to entertain prospective clients. You got lucky enough to stumble in at just the right time."

"I guess I did. Truth be told, I couldn't really believe it. It was kind of surreal, finding that sort of party behind a shitty bar like that."

He nodded. "Yeah, we get that a lot. We've actually owned that building for nearly a century. It's where the company started. As we expanded, we decided to upgrade it and turn it into a space for entertaining. There's still a few of the old offices left, one of which I believe you are somewhat acquainted with."

My cheeks heated. I wondered if I'd ever live that down.

"So why keep the bar at the front?" I asked. "Why not knock it down and build something nicer? You can obviously afford to."

He shrugged. "Call it sentimentality I guess. That bar's been there since the building was built. It's nice to keep a small piece of the old place around."

There was nothing in his voice to hint at any deception. Perhaps there really was nothing more to it. It was certainly the simplest explanation. Of course there were still the things the girl had told me that morning, and the papers on his desk, but were they really as odd as they seemed? It was hardly strange to want a little privacy, and I hadn't really had more than a few furtive seconds with that document. It was verging on paranoid to make any assumptions based on that. I decided to give him the benefit of the doubt.

A minute later, we arrived at the restaurant. It was a glorious sight. The whole building was a giant glass cylinder, offering a full panoramic view of Circular Quay. A suited maître d' led us to a table on the upper floor, which was right next to the window facing out across the water to the Opera House. The sun had just finished setting and the whole bay was bathed in the soft glow of the city lights from the south. It was a spectacular location.

The two chairs at the table were opposite one another, but after helping me into my seat, he took his and lifted it around, sitting right next to me, his leg brushing softly against mine. My heart quickened. In the blink of an eye, he'd made the whole meal feel much more intimate.

"I can't imagine why anyone would cancel on this," I said, watching as one of the night ferries pulled out of the dock, sending great ripples rolling through the harbour. "It's beautiful."

"I like everything about this place," he said. "I try to come as often as possible. The only thing better than the food is the view." He gave me an exaggerated look up and down. "And I must say, the view is looking particularly spectacular tonight."

I grinned and returned the leer. "It's not so bad from over here either."

Our menus arrived. If it wasn't already obvious, the service quickly made it clear that this wasn't just any lazy Sunday meal. Our waitress was polite, articulate and immaculately groomed. She knew the menu back to front and answered every question Sebastian asked, quickly and in great detail. While they spoke, a second waiter arrived, filling our water glasses and leaving a small basket of steaming bread for us to nibble on.

Sebastian wanted to order the nine course tasting menu, but I'd had bad experiences with that sort of food in the past.

"It always seems a little too pretentious for its own good," I told him.

"Trust me."

And so I relented.

The first course arrived almost instantly, a plate containing two 'Sea Pearls'; delicate spheres about the size of ping pong balls. They didn't look like much, but had the most amazing silky texture and they just melted to nothing in my mouth.

"So, how long have you been with Little Bell?" he asked. Apparently even outsiders knew about our little nickname.

"Just over six years now."

"You like it?"

I shrugged. "It's a great company. They do some really fantastic work and there's lots of variation."

"I'm sensing there's a 'but' coming."

I sighed. I hadn't really planned on whining to him on our first date, but he seemed genuinely interested, and I was sick of bottling up all my frustration. "But I'm starting to feel like it's a dead end."

"Why?"

"It just seems like if something was going to happen for me there it already would have. There aren't many people there who work harder than me, but no matter how much I bust my ass for them, I can't seem to make any progress."

He took a sip of wine. "So why not move somewhere where they respect your talents?"

"I don't know. It would make the last few years feel like a waste, I guess. I hate giving up. Once I start something, I tend to stick to it until I get the job done. Besides, Little Bell is one of the best in the business. If I can make it there, that's a big deal."

"Well, it depends on why you became a lawyer doesn't it?

If what you're interested in is 'making it' — and there's no shame in having that as a goal — then yeah, I'd say you're in the right place. But if you're doing it because it's what you love to do, then you might find yourself wasted there."

"What if it's a little of both?"

"That's where it gets tricky," he said with a smile.

"Don't get me wrong, I enjoy what I do," I continued. "And it's not that I care about image or status. I just like a challenge, you know? I want to prove to myself I can do it."

"That's something I can relate to. Sometimes I think I go out of my way to make things difficult for myself, just so it's more fun when I finally get there."

"Exactly," I said. "I've thought about leaving, but it would just be such a big risk, starting over again from scratch."

"Nothing worth having comes risk free."

The second course arrived. Objectively, it was probably as good as the first, but I wasn't paying much attention. Instead, I was rolling Sebastian's words around in my mind. This sort of discussion wasn't what I'd expected from him. Maybe I'd just been blinded by his initial approach, but I'd assumed our table talk would be a little lighter; a flirtatious game of back and forth. Instead, we'd ventured into a real conversation, and Sebastian was proving to be an excellent sounding board. He was honest, intelligent and articulate. It was a strange feeling, realising the two dimensional cut out in my head was deeper than I thought.

"So what about you? You enjoy working at Fraiser?" I asked.

There was a small pause. "It's great," he said with a nod. "I honestly couldn't imagine being anywhere else."

"Well, with the way they seem to take care of their employees, I can't say I'm surprised."

He chuckled. "We work as hard as we play, but they're good to us, yeah."

"I get the sense that they can afford to be."

He shrugged. "We've backed some strong horses recently. It's paid off."

"So that's what it's about then? 'Backing horses'? Sorry, I don't know much about venture capitalism. For me, it's always fallen under the umbrella of 'miscellaneous financial jobs that all seem vaguely the same'."

His indulgent expression said that was a common perception. "Well, in a nutshell, we take people's money and invest it in projects we think might be profitable. Some work out, some don't. We split the profits and losses with our investors."

"Is that what you did for Chase Adams?" The words left my mouth before I could stop them. I hadn't realised it, but that connection was still bothering me.

He did a double take, looking startled for a brief second, but it was gone again in an instant. "Ah, I'd forgotten he was there the other night. Well, to put it simply, yes. He's been a long standing client of ours."

"And now he just comes by and parties with you guys?"

"When he's in town."

I wouldn't have picked a Hollywood A-Lister to spend his time hanging with a bunch of corporate types, no matter how much cash they'd made him, but perhaps I was underestimating them. "So, you guys deal with some pretty big names then. Anyone else I might have heard of?"

He shot me a little smile. "Probably, but all of them would be quite upset if I began talking about their investments in public."

I tried my best to hide my disappointment. Stonewalled again. "Well, it doesn't sound like such a bad deal really," I said. "Getting paid to party with clients and throw huge sums of money around to see what sticks."

He looked amused. "It's a little more complicated than that." But he didn't elaborate further. Apparently, he took his bosses' penchant for secrecy to heart. Learning anything about him was going to be a slow process.

I watched him as he ate. Even doing that, there was an economic grace to his movements that was a joy to behold. It set my mind wandering, imaging what he might look like doing other things.

He caught me staring and grinned, exposing a row of perfect teeth. "And what are you looking at?"

I blushed, somehow sure he knew exactly what I'd been thinking. "Nothing."

"My mistake then," he said.

The third course arrived. Some kind of creamy crab dish that tasted so fresh I wouldn't have been surprised to learn it had been pulled from the sea just minutes earlier.

"So are you enjoying dinner?" he asked me, after we'd both scraped our bowls clean.

I nodded. "I was a little sceptical, but this place definitely lives up to its reputation. My only problem is, I'm not sure what I'm going to do once it's over. You might have ruined me for homemade spag bol and cheap Chinese forever now."

His mouth quirked up ever so slightly. "I have a few ideas about what we could do once it's over."

Wow. Again. He never missed an opening. "I'm sure you do," I said, keeping my voice neutral, "but I don't remember agreeing to anything beyond dinner."

"No you didn't." *But you will*, his eyes finished. A strange sensation rolled through my chest, and I looked away. I didn't know how to fight that, that unrelenting certainty. I'd done everything in my power to resist, and I'd still wound up at dinner with him. What chance did I have of stopping him now?

"Nonetheless, I'm glad you came," he continued. "For a while I was sure I'd scared you off.

"Your approach was a little... unorthodox."

He laughed. "Perhaps. But nothing about this—" he gestured to the space between us "—is orthodox."

"You mean you don't routinely pick up girls you find hiding in your wardrobe?" I joked, trying to guide the conversation back to lighter territory. If things turned any more risqué, I knew I'd be in trouble.

But he wasn't having any of it. "Surprisingly, I think that's a first," he said, his voice growing huskier. He reached out and ran a finger softly along my arm, coming to rest on my hand. "But I can honestly say I've never been so pleased to have my privacy intruded upon before."

And just like that, the tension in the air was back. It settled over my skin like a fine mist. I knew I should find something to say, but as always, his touch left my mind flailing.

"You know, I wanted you from the moment you first walked in through that door the other night, Sophia."

"You did?" I asked, my voice reed thin.

He nodded. "All I could think about after our first discussion was what it would be like to take you home with me. To watch your body tremble as I made you come."

The way he brazenly ventured into such erotic territory was disarming, and quite frankly hot as hell. I knew I should probably have been offended, but all I could think about was letting him do exactly what he'd just described.

"To have you like that would have been enough," he continued. "But after finding you crouched in my office, watching me spank Hannah, I realised something." He reached out and brushed my chin, guiding my eyes to his. "You want more than that too."

"I don't... I mean, we're not—" a single finger pressed into my lips, silencing me, teasing my mouth with hints of salt and musk.

"When I found you kneeling on the floor that night, you were practically radiating excitement. I could smell your arousal. You want this Sophia, you want to do more than just watch, and I'm going to be the one that shows you."

His gaze bored into me with steely promise. I felt myself growing hot. It was unsettling, hearing him say those things, giving voice to the fears that had been simmering inside me. That night had been a flurry of confusion and alien sensations. I still couldn't wrap my head around the idea of giving yourself to someone so completely. It felt too much like being taken advantage of, like being used. But if that was the case, why was my body so flushed with desire?

"I'm sure it works for some people," I stammered, "but I just don't think that's me."

"Who are you trying to fool?" he asked, his eyes ablaze. "You wouldn't have come tonight unless you were curious. It was always going to come to this. We'll go slowly, as slowly as you like, but you're coming home with me, and I promise you that by the end, you'll be begging for more."

My heart was hammering in my chest. Something told me this decision was important. I could say no, and things would simply return to normal. But then I'd never know for sure. Did I really want to spend my life asking 'what if?'

"Okay," I said, my voice barely more than a whisper.

He let out a long breath, the sigh of a man who had just gotten everything he ever wanted. Instantly he signalled the waitress. "I can't wait until after dinner. I need to be inside you now."

I trembled, feeling myself grow wet at the mere suggestion. I nodded. Food was suddenly the last thing on my mind.

The cheque arrived and he paid for the full meal without blinking. It was an astronomical sum for what amounted to a few sips and bites, but he didn't seem to care.

We made our way outside, but as I turned to head back to the car, he grabbed me by the arm.

"What—" I started to say, but in an instant I was spinning back towards him and his lips were on mine. In that kiss, I saw a prelude of what was to come. It was as strong and intoxicating as the man himself. He crushed his face against mine, sandwiching my body between his chest and the glass behind. His tongue explored my mouth greedily, darting and teasing, while his fingers prowled along my shoulders, my back, and the nape of my neck. I kissed back as best I could, but I felt a little like a shell on the beach, struggling not to get swept out by the tide. He was so powerful, so determined, and my body seemed to turn boneless in his hands. All I could really do was stand there and *be* kissed. It wasn't just an expression of passion, but one of possession. And it felt sinfully good.

I could feel a throbbing hardness building against my stomach as he ground himself against me. An intense pang of desire rushed through me, pooling between my legs.

What felt like a lifetime later, he broke away. "Jesus," he said, his voice ragged. "I'm not sure I should have done that."

"Why not?"

"Now I don't know if I can last the car ride home."

"Well," I said, running my hand gently down his stomach and coming to rest on the tip of his impressive bulge. "You said we could take it slow. 'As slow as you like,' I believe were your words. And I'd like to wait." In truth, I was almost at breaking point myself. If he'd carried me into the bathroom and bent me over then and there I'm not sure I'd have been able to object, but I was enjoying that rare moment of power over him.

He drew a sharp, shuddering breath and closed his eyes briefly, before seizing my wrist and pulling my arm away. "Then that's what we'll do," he said, a strained smile on his face. "But you should know, I have ways of dealing with girls who like to tease."

"I'm sure you do," I replied, thinking back to Hannah's raw ass. Strangely, in my aroused state, I didn't find the image as intimidating as I once had.

Chapter 8

We walked briskly over to where the limo was parked. "Home," Sebastian said to Joe, before ushering me into the back. He wore the determined look of the man on a very important mission. I wondered if Joe understood what was about to take place. After ten years, he likely had a good grasp of his boss's habits, so the answer was probably yes. Normally, that might have bothered me, but at that moment I was too turned on to care.

The car ride to Sebastian's house only took ten minutes, but it felt much longer. He didn't speak. His silence seemed almost meditative, so I didn't interrupt. I just stared out the window and considered what I was getting myself into.

Eventually, we pulled up outside a sleek white apartment building that looked out over Woolloomooloo Bay. The harbour was quiet at night, but I could still hear the gentle crash of waves breaking against the hulls of the moored yachts that lined the docks.

We said farewell to Joe and then Sebastian took my hand and led me inside. I thought the car ride might have cooled his excitement a little, but as soon as the lift doors closed behind us, he was on me once more. He kissed me with a hunger that was almost strong enough to be frightening, pinning me against the metal wall and driving his mouth onto mine. Free from any wandering eyes, his hands lost whatever sense of propriety they'd once had, running up my sides before sliding down to caress the curves of my ass. I moaned, half in pleasure half in protest, but there was no one to see, and no way to stop the relentless onslaught that was Sebastian Lock.

Seizing me more firmly, he lifted me up until our mouths were at the same height. I took the opportunity to loop my arms and legs around him and run my fingers through the black tangle of his hair, pulling him closer still. My dress was beginning to ride up, and the change in height pushed the pulsing mass of his cock directly against my dripping panties. He let out a growl and began to rock back and forward, using the lift wall as leverage.

"God, you're so wet. I can feel it even through our clothes."

"This is what you do to me," I said, my voice trembling.

He brought one huge hand up and wrapped it around my chin, raising my eyes to his. "No, this is just a taste of what I can do to you. There is so much more. All I've been able to think about since we met was making you come. I'm going to do it in a thousand ways, ways you didn't even know existed."

"God yes," I breathed, already able to feel an orgasm beckoning in the distance. The pressure of his crotch against mine was amazing, and his mouth was now doing divine things to my neck, kissing and nibbling in slow circles. The coarse brush of his stubble against my skin sent waves of sensation rolling through me, like the gentle scrape of sand on the wind.

I assumed we'd have to walk down some kind of corridor, but the lift opened straight into Sebastian's apartment. Without even breaking our embrace, he spun and carried me through the doorway. Pressed against him like that I could feel the taut strength of his muscles flex and shift as we moved. He held me as easily as a child. I couldn't wait to see the body that lay beneath those clothes. I could already picture it, all hard slabs and trembling sinew.

Entwined as we were, I barely noticed my surroundings. Sebastian navigated us expertly to the bedroom, never breaking our kiss for more than a moment. There was something so primal about being carried off to be ravished. I felt claimed, taken, possessed. It was an intensely erotic experience.

Throwing me down onto the bed, he climbed on top of me. My hands now free, I reached up eagerly for his shirt buttons, but he caught both my wrists in one hand. "You said you wanted to wait," he said, his voice teasing.

I started to protest, but his expression silenced me. "Before we go any further," he continued, "I want to establish some ground rules. I told you that we could go slowly, and I meant it. But nonetheless, it's important to me that everything we do is consensual. So with that in mind, you need to pick a safe word. Something distinctive that will never come up under normal circumstances. If what we're doing ever gets too much, you just utter that word and I promise everything stops. No questions asked. Understand?"

I nodded. At that particular moment he could have been asking me for my bank account number and PIN and I'd probably have given them.

"So, pick a word."

Surprisingly, one came to me instantly. "Cinderella."

He looked at me curiously. "That's an... odd choice."

He was right. I had no idea why I'd picked that, although it did make me realise I still hadn't gotten my shoes back. *Some fairy tale this is.*

"I'll explain later," I told him impatiently.

"Fair enough. Cinderella it is." He leaned in, planting a

soft kiss just below my ear. "And now, Sophia, I want to taste you."

I squirmed against him, those words amping the fire inside me up to fever pitch. I felt like my body couldn't possibly maintain that state of arousal for much longer, like I was prepped to burst at any minute. "Please."

Releasing my hands, he slid down the bed and shoved my skirt up around my hips. There was no preamble. He didn't even take the time to undress me. He simply tugged my panties aside and then his tongue was on my pussy.

"Oh...fuck." That first touch was like electricity, sending a wave of pleasure sizzling through me. Another joined it, curling around the first, and then another. Soon, I could feel nothing else save the vortex roaring inside me.

It seemed he'd been serious when he said he wanted to taste me. Rather than focus on my clit straight away like I'd expected, he worked the length of me, caressing my dripping opening with long, soft strokes and occasionally slipping inside to fuck me with his tongue.

"My god, you're so sweet," he said. "You're just as delicious as I'd imagined."

I could only moan in reply, grinding myself against him. I felt like I was coming apart at the seams, like every stroke, every lick was peeling away just a little more of me.

I reached out to take his head in my hands, desperate to pull him even closer, but again he seized my wrists. "No hands. Your pleasure is mine to control. I was going to save the ties for another night, but if you can't learn to behave, I'll have to bind you now."

My stomach twisted at the thought of being restrained. I'd be utterly at his mercy.

"I'll be good," I said, my voice soft.

"Excellent." He released me.

His hands now free, he brought one down and slid a long finger inside of me, tenderly stroking my G-spot while his tongue began licking a delicate figure eight across my swollen bud.

"Fuck you're tight. And so soft. God, it's killing me that I'm not inside of you right now."

"So fuck me," I said, the words barely recognisable. I wanted him more than I could remember wanting anything before. I was nearly delirious with desire.

"Soon, but first I want to watch you come. I want to feel you tighten around my fingers. And I want you to think about the fact that this is just the first of many. This is but the tiniest scrap of the things we can do together."

I writhed against the sheet, certain it wouldn't be long before he got his wish. I could already feel my muscles tensing, preparing for that explosion that would tear through me.

"Oh god, oh fuck," I cried, crossing the point of no return. My body buckled and my vision shattered as I rocked against him. Wordless sounds spilt from my mouth, animal sounds, sounds I'd never heard myself make before. And the whole time he gazed into my eyes, primal satisfaction painted on his face.

As my senses finally returned, I heard the snicker of a zipper being unfastened. "Oh no, not yet, I'm too sensitive and it's been so long. Just a few minutes," I whispered.

"I have to have you, Sophia. Now. I can't wait any longer." His voice sounded pained. He produced a condom from somewhere. "Are you on birth control?"

"Yes."

He tore it open. "Good. Next time, I'll prove that I'm clean. You'll do the same. And then we'll be able to dispense with these. I don't want anything between us in the future."

I nodded slowly, still unsure I'd be able to take him yet,

but one look at his face told me there was no stopping him now. He didn't even pause to remove his shirt. I caught the barest flash of hot olive skin as his pants hit the floor, then he was pressing himself slowly inside me. "Oh Jesus, Sophia," he groaned.

Even without seeing it, I could tell his cock was huge. The stretching sensation in those first few moments was almost overpowering, and my tender skin burned in protest. But my body had taken on a life of its own at that point. My muscles began to flex and ripple, hungrily drawing him in. I felt myself growing wetter still, and gradually the discomfort faded, replaced by a divine sense of fullness.

Once again I found my hands wandering, dancing across his chest. His muscles were taut beneath the soft cotton of his shirt. Unable to restrain myself, I traced my fingers up toward the collar and slipped inside, savouring the warmth and slickness of his skin. He allowed this for a few seconds, but then his hands caught mine once more, pinning them to the pillow above. Before I could object, he leaned down, sealing his lips over mine, his tongue shooting in to claim another part of me.

With his weight on top of me and my arms held, I couldn't move. I could only lie there as he had his way with me. I felt a rush of excitement. That sense of powerlessness was strangely intoxicating.

"That's it, I want you to take all of me," he said, his cock now deep inside me.

"God yes. Keep going," I replied, rocking my hips back and forward, easing him deeper still.

As I finally adjusted to his size, he began to fuck me harder. His body crushed against mine, grinding my clit while his cock hammered my G-spot. The sensation was exquisite. As impossible as it seemed, I could feel another orgasm rearing up inside me.

He was clearly not far away either. His breath was coming in little spurts and there was a low growl emanating from his throat. I loved that sound. I could feel it vibrating all the way through his body and into mine; another declaration of his possessive intent.

His hips worked like an out of control piston, steadily gaining force. His thrusts became wilder and his fingers tightened, digging into my skin. Leaning down, he brought his face just inches from mine.

"I'm going to come, Sophia," he panted.

"Oh fuck, give it to me."

My words seemed to send him over the edge. With one final mighty pump, he exploded inside me. His back arched and his eyes flared as my pussy clenched around him, milking every drop.

That sudden rush of heat was too much, and with another cry I came too. I hadn't thought it possible, but this orgasm was even more intense. It tore through my body like a tidal wave, curling my toes and leaving me breathless and limp.

When we were both spent, we collapsed onto the bed together. I was pleased to see he looked as drained as I did; face flushed, body slick with sweat.

Lying there nestled against him was lovely. I'd forgotten what it felt like to have a pair of strong arms wrapped around me. It was a surprisingly tender gesture, like what we'd just shared had stripped away a little of that professional armour.

"Wow," I said, when I could finally speak again.

He gave a short laugh. "My thoughts exactly. God, that was intense." His brow crinkled. "It wasn't too much was it? I wanted to take it slow, really. I didn't mean to grab you, but once I had you underneath me like that, I lost control."

I thought back to that rush of adrenaline when he'd seized my hands. It scared me to admit, but perhaps he was right.

81

Perhaps there were a few things I didn't know about myself. "No. In fact, when you pinned me down, I kind of liked that. It felt so... animal."

A huge smile split his face. "I was hoping you'd say that." He ran a hand gently down my naked ass, that emerald gaze searing into me. "Because now that I've had a taste of you, I don't think I can stop. There are so many things I want to show you."

I drew a deep breath. I didn't know exactly what I was committing to, but I wasn't sure I had a choice anymore. The strange hunger Sebastian had awakened inside me wasn't going away. It had started that first night crouched in the wardrobe, and tonight had been like pouring fuel on a fire. "Well, I think I want to be shown," I said, my voice shaking. "Slowly," I added, having sudden visions of him carrying me off, wrapping me in leather and chaining me in the basement.

"With you, I have absolutely no objections to taking my time." It sounded like both a threat and a promise. I suspected that whatever pace we moved at, the experience would be something special.

I licked my lips. I wasn't sure exactly what the typical rules of such arrangements were, but certain things still bothered me. "I have a condition though."

He looked amused. "Oh?"

"What we do stays strictly in the bedroom. Hannah may have let you control other parts of her life, but that's not me. Everywhere but in here, I'm my own person."

His smile grew. "Honestly, I wouldn't have expected anything else. Submission is different for everyone. It's an intensely personal thing. For Hannah, discipline was important, so I gave her what she needed." He ran a hand gently up my side. "But I'm perfectly happy just having your body in here."

"That sounds about perfect to me," I replied, savouring

the sensation of his touch. "Oh and one other thing. There will be none of that 'Sir' stuff. Like, ever. That seriously weirds me out."

He laughed. "Alright. Noted."

We lay for a few moments in silence.

"This was a lovely night," I said eventually. "It's been a long time since I went on a date; especially one that escalated this quickly."

His expression fell ever so slightly. "I'm glad you enjoyed yourself." He paused, as if choosing his words carefully. "But you know it won't be like this all the time, right? This—" he gestured to the bed "—I can give you, but I can't promise much more than that."

I nodded slowly. I had no illusions about the sort of man he was, and what he was proposing should have been exactly what I wanted; all the fun of a relationship and none of the fuss. But nonetheless, his candour made me a little uneasy. It was still difficult to wrap my head around the idea that I wasn't being taken advantage of.

"I know," I replied, trying to act nonplussed. "It was just nice to spend a night doing things the old fashioned way, you know? Most days I barely have time to scoff down a bowl of two minute noodles."

He relaxed a little. "That makes two of us."

We lay for a few minutes in silence. In an attempt to distract myself, I began to explore his body. He was still clothed from the waist up, but this time he didn't stop me as I slipped my hand beneath his shirt. I ran my fingers gently over his skin, admiring the smooth, hard curves beneath. And then I noticed something I hadn't seen before.

"Wow. You didn't strike me as a tattoo kind of guy," I said, hopping onto my elbows to get a closer look. Neatly inscribed on the right side of his chest, was an ornate letter A.

Something about the image looked vaguely familiar, but I couldn't place it. "What's it stand for?"

He hesitated. "Nothing really. Call it a relic from my younger and stupider days." He rolled slightly onto his side and reached up my skirt to cup my ass. "You know, if you keep touching me like that, you're just asking for trouble."

With his body pressed up against me, I could feel a throbbing presence begin to jut into my thigh. He was growing hard again. All other thoughts fled my mind.

I peeled back the sheet and his cock sprang into view. It was the first time I'd really gotten a good look at it. Long and almost as thick as my wrist, it had two large veins wrapped around it like decorations. Warmth gushed through me once more. I couldn't believe I'd had that inside me. It seemed impossibly big.

I'd always been a once-and-done kind of girl. I'd assumed I simply wasn't built for multiple orgasms. But Sebastian had already managed to shatter that illusion tonight, and now, against all odds, I found my body stirring once more. He had that look in his eye again; that raw, carnal need that I couldn't help but respond to.

I reached out to stroke the length of him. "Is that so?" I said. "Well, I think there's only one way I'm going to learn."

Chapter 9

My second time with Sebastian was even more tiring than the first, and when he finally dropped me home, I fell asleep almost instantly. I had no idea how he managed such virility. He seemed to have the stamina of ten men. Not that I was complaining.

I woke feeling refreshed, a pleasant ache between my legs. I assumed I'd get used to marathon sex sessions eventually, but for now, my body was not accustomed to such vigour. Thinking back to the four toe curling orgasms I'd had, I decided a little soreness was a fair price to pay.

My day at the office started with a floor wide strategy meeting. Normally our work was delegated across a mixture of small meetings, phone calls and emails, but whenever we began a big case like Wrights, we needed a little more coordination. I was excited to finally have something important to sink my teeth into.

After a less than rousing speech from Alan, the senior Partner who ran our floor, about the importance of "obtaining justice for those that might otherwise slip through the cracks," we got down to business.

Work was gradually parcelled out, with everyone heading off to begin their assigned tasks. Soon, there were only a few people left in the room.

"As for the rest of you," Alan said, "we need you to hold down the fort with the rest of our case load for now. Wrights is important, but it's not the only thing on our books."

Those words were like a punch in the stomach. Again I was being relegated to the bench.

It wasn't considered proper to object about your duties, but I was sick of playing second fiddle to people with less dedication and experience than me.

"Excuse me, sir," I said to Alan, as the others were filing out. I didn't know him well, but he had a reputation for being difficult to deal with, so I wanted to tread carefully.

"Yes Sophia, what is it?"

"I just wanted to talk to you about my assignment. To be honest I'm kind of disappointed not to be working on the Wrights case."

He shot me a sympathetic smile, but it lacked any real warmth. "I know it's not ideal, but we need people on our other cases too."

"I know. It's just there are plenty of less experienced associates working on the case. I think I can be more useful there than here."

His lips tightened. "Nobody doubts your talents, Sophia. They're the reason we've got you doing this. We need someone with your kind of experience keeping things on track elsewhere. You'll get your chance on the Wrights case soon enough, don't worry."

It was a classic Partner trick; act like the shitty job you've just doled out is more important than it actually is. But there wasn't anything I else I could really do. The only person who might consider helping was my direct boss Ernest, and Alan outranked him.

I thanked him and headed back to my desk.

With the majority of the floor now occupied with the new case, my morning quickly grew hectic. Phone calls and emails streamed in, never giving me time to catch my breath. I was so set in my rhythm, that when a call arrived around one o'clock, I didn't even notice that it was from a familiar number.

"Sophia Pearce," I said, doing nothing to hide the strain in my voice.

"Well hello to you too." I recognised Ruth's voice instantly.

"Shit, sorry. Kind of busy here. Thought you were another fucking client who didn't know his ass from his elbow. What's up?"

"What's up is that I'm downstairs."

"Why wou—ah shit."

She exhaled loudly. "I take it that means you forgot?"

"Possibly."

"This was your idea, for Christ's sake. 'Come have lunch on Monday,' you said. 'We'll catch up, just the two of us.'"

"I know. I'm sorry. I'm just really busy today and it slipped my mind."

"Well, I can wait a few. Finish up what you're doing and come down."

"I don't know, Ruth. I've got a mountain of stuff to do here—"

"Even mountaineers need to eat. Come on, I came all the way across town. The least you can do is give me half an hour. We'll go to Pablo's."

It was my turn to sigh. Ruth wasn't going to give up. And as much as I knew I should power on, the thought of escaping, even for a little while, was very appealing. "Okay fine. Give me five."

"Atta girl. I'll be out front."

Fifteen minutes later we were climbing down a narrow staircase and into a dimly lit basement. Pablo's was one of my favourite restaurants. It had the perfect combination of up-market panache and homely comfort food. The tables around us were piled high with steaming olive rolls and mounds of bolognese, while waistcoated waiters darted nimbly between them like insects, ensuring the glasses of wine and sparkling water never quite reached empty.

More than a few men's eyes followed us as we walked. I sometimes liked to pretend that those stares were for me, but the truth was, whenever Ruth was in a room, it was all eyes on her. There was just something about her that men couldn't resist. She wasn't stunningly beautiful — she had a little too much of her mother's sharp nose for that — but she had a way of moving that just exuded sexuality. Men seemed to melt in her presence; a fact she took ample advantage of.

"So, how are the unhappy couples of Sydney treating you?" I asked, once we'd ordered. Ruth was a family law attorney, specialising in messy divorce.

"No complaints. Things are a little quiet, but that's just the calm before the post-Christmas storm."

"Post-Christmas storm?"

"Yea. Haven't you noticed I'm always super busy come January?"

I thought about it. "Sure, I guess. But why?"

"Two words. Christmas parties. Unlimited booze, no spouses, lots of mistletoe; it's like divorce lawyer heaven."

I laughed. "Good to see you're still bringing that notorious professional sensitivity to the table."

She raised her hands defensively. "Hey, ninety percent of the time the divorcee is getting what they deserve. I've got a couple of doozeys right now." She leaned in close. "This one poor guy just found out that his wife was cheating on him...

with his dad."

"No shit?"

Ruth shook her head. "But it gets worse. They have a kid, about four years old. Paternity tests just came back."

"Not his?"

She shook her head.

"Fuck."

"Exactly. The guy has been raising his own brother. You couldn't make this shit up if you tried. It's like an episode of Jerry Springer. But anyway, enough about my sordid little life. I've already said too much. How are things on your end?"

"Fine, fine, just busy."

She gazed at me for a second. "You look tired, Soph. Busy doesn't mean you can't get a proper night's sleep every once in a while."

I rolled my eyes. "Yes mum."

"I'm serious! You can't keep working yourself into the ground."

"It's not like it's intentional. Sometimes there's just too much to do. We just landed a really big case, so I doubt things will let up any time soon."

"Is that Wrights? The one you were telling me about?"

"Yep."

"Well, that's awesome!" She noticed my resigned expression. "Right?"

"It would be if I was actually working on it."

She blew out a long puff of air. If anybody knew about my frustrations at work, it was Ruth. "They're seriously not using you at all?"

I shrugged. "Not so far. It's early days yet, and Alan said I'd be rotated in, so maybe I'm just being bitter. I'm just so sick of sitting on the sidelines."

"I know. They're idiots for wasting you like that." She

89

reached out and squeezed my hand. "But eventually someone there is going to recognise how fucking great you are at your job, and when that happens, the sky's the limit."

That drew a smile from me. Ruth was always wonderful at cheering me up. "Thanks."

"No problem." Her expression turned cheeky. "You know if you want, we could go out tonight. Lou is away at her mum's, so it would just be us two single gals. Maybe we could find ourselves a couple of willing young gentlemen to take our minds off our troubles?"

I sucked in a sharp breath. I'd really been hoping the conversation wouldn't go down that path, but I should have known better with Ruth. I wasn't sure how to respond. I hated the idea of lying to my friend, but I didn't feel comfortable talking about Sebastian just yet. I barely had a handle on the way he made me feel. I didn't need the challenge of trying to describe it to someone else.

I opened my mouth to brush her off, but I must have waited a beat too long, because suddenly her eyes lit up. "You sneaky little hussy! You're already getting some right now, aren't you?" I turned red. "Yeah, busy with work indeed. You're busy getting banged all night long. No wonder you look so tired."

There wasn't much point in lying now. The jig was up. "I wouldn't describe us as busy exactly. We only just met." A small grin slipped onto my face. "It did last most of the night though."

Ruth laughed. "That's a promising start. Well, don't keep me in suspense. Who is this mystery Casanova?"

"Well, remember the other night when I snuck into that party..." I trailed off, waiting for Ruth to fill in the blanks.

It didn't take long. "Oh, you didn't? You did!" She laughed. "That guy you were telling us about? How? When?"

And so I told the story. In typical Ruth fashion, she did her best to extract the more pornographic details, but I managed to keep Sebastian's kinkiness largely under wraps.

"Sounds like quite a guy," she said when I was done.

I nodded slowly. "That he is. Honestly, it's a little intimidating. Every time I'm around him I seem to lose my head completely."

She flashed a knowing smile. "They're dangerous when they're that gorgeous."

"It's not just his looks." I shook my head. "I don't know if I can really explain it. There's just something about him that pushes all my buttons."

"Is it the accent? Fuck, I love a good accent." She leaned back in her chair and gazed up at the ceiling, a dreamy grin blooming on her face. "Remember that Spanish guy I was seeing a year or so back? God damn. He could read out the shopping list and I'd still get off."

"You did mention he had a talented tongue, but I didn't think that's what you meant."

She laughed. "That man had a variety of skills, most of which cannot be discussed in polite company. Anyway, it sounds like you're living the dream. Exclusive, casual sex with a gorgeous, mysterious millionaire. I dare say I'm a little envious."

"Yea it's pretty awesome." I tried my best to sound enthusiastic, but some part of my uncertainty must have leaked through, because her expression fell.

"So why don't you sound happy?" she asked.

"I am!" I sighed. It was frustrating how little I could hide from her. Who said best friends were a good idea anyway? "It's just, I'm kind of waiting for the other shoe to drop, you know?"

"Jesus. You really know how to look a gift horse in the

mouth, don't you?"

"I'm not trying to. I just want to keep things in perspective. After what happened with Connor, I want to be a little more careful, that's all."

She grimaced and leaned in close, taking my hands in her. "Soph, listen to me. Connor was a one of a kind psychopath. He was a serial cheater who seemed to get off on lying to you. I've told you before, men might be assholes sometimes, but he was a special piece of work. They aren't all like that. You can't let that one experience cause you to shut up shop forever."

I nodded slowly. "I know."

"You need something to do besides work and drink, and if you ask me, this sounds perfect. A casual fling with a guy who is as busy as you are. Just take it slow and enjoy it for what it is."

"That's the plan."

"Good." She took a drink and then shook her head. "I swear, you don't know how lucky you are. This sort of thing doesn't come along all that often."

I thought back to our bizarre courtship. In the rational light of day, it barely seemed plausible at all. "I think I agree with you there."

Chapter 10

The next few days were uneventful. A little of the Wrights case work trickled down to me, but nothing significant. I debated confronting Alan again, but I got the sense I'd already made a mistake complaining the first time. Pushing any more was likely to just make the situation worse. So instead, I swallowed my pride and focused on the tasks that were given to me.

I didn't hear anything from Sebastian. When we'd parted, we'd made no concrete plans to see each other again and that was fine with me. After all, what was the point of a casual fling if it filled your diary with obligations?

But as the days became a week, I began to grow uneasy. I wasn't expecting daily phone calls, but it felt like there should be some kind of communication. To make matters worse, I realised that I had no way of contacting him. I might have been able to find his building again if I really wanted to, but he'd never given me his phone number or even an email address. Our relationship effectively existed entirely on his whim.

"It's partially my fault I guess," I said to Ruth on the phone one night. "I should have asked for his number. But that doesn't make the situation any better. It's like I'm just lying around waiting until he feels like fucking me again."

"Isn't that what a casual relationship is?" she asked.

"I guess," I replied slowly, "but it's not supposed to be this one sided. What if *I* decide I'm in the mood?"

She laughed. "Feeling a little hot under the collar are we?"

As much as I hated to admit it, I was. My sex drive had never been much more than a low buzz in the background before, but my one night with Sebastian seemed to have kick started my libido something fierce. I found my eyes wandering much more than they used to, and my dreams had taken a notably erotic turn. It was quite inconvenient really.

"Maybe a little."

"Well," she continued, "I'm sure he didn't keep his number hidden on purpose. Just ask for it next time."

Knowing the sort of man Sebastian was, it wouldn't have surprised me if it had been intentional, but I didn't argue.

"What really bothers me is... what if there isn't a next time?" I said. "What if my gut was right and he was just looking for an easy lay?"

"A few days of silence is hardly a big deal. This is what you signed up for, remember? No fuss."

"I guess," I said again.

"And if it turns out he did take advantage of you, then yea he's an asshole, but worrying isn't going to change anything. Think of it this way; there are far worse things than one night stands with handsome foreign gentlemen who are great in bed."

I laughed. Ruth certainly knew how to put things in perspective.

I tried my best to take her advice to heart, but as more time passed, my restlessness grew. What was the threshold for when that sort of behaviour became unacceptable? Two weeks? A month? I had no idea. It felt like he'd gone to a lot of trouble just to sleep with me once and then drop me, but the evidence was growing increasingly hard to ignore.

Then one day nearly three weeks later, when I'd basically given up hope of ever seeing him again, I returned from a lunch meeting to find my office door open. Sebastian was leaning casually against my desk, suited, chiselled, and looking as dapper as ever.

"Seriously?" I hissed. Under other circumstances I might have reacted more calmly, but the way he stood there, smiling like his presence was totally normal, made my blood run hot.

"Still haven't got those greetings down pat yet, have you?" he replied, looking bemused at my dark expression.

"That's really the best you can do?"

"I'm not sure what else you were hoping for."

I strode into the room, slamming the door behind me. "I don't hear anything from you for three weeks, then you think it's okay to just show up at my office when the mood finally strikes you?"

His jaw tightened. "I didn't realise I owed you minute by minute updates of everything I did."

"You don't. You don't owe me anything. I guess I just hoped you might *want* to check in on me. A text message every once in a while isn't a big ask."

"It's not that I don't want to. I've just been busy." He began pacing. "I thought we understood one another, Sophia."

"So did I, but apparently I didn't make myself clear. That one dinner doesn't give you license to just ignore me until you feel like getting laid again."

"That's not how it is."

"Well that's how it seems to me."

He exhaled slowly. "I thought you were okay with keeping things simple."

"Simple is fine. Simple is great. I don't need romantic dates or bloody hand crafted mix tapes, but I do need to feel like I'm more than just a walking vagina that operates at your beck and call."

He studied me for several seconds, his expression growing concerned. "I'm sorry. I never meant to make you feel that way," he said in a soft voice.

I felt some of my rage draining away. He looked genuinely distressed at having hurt me, although that didn't change the fact that he had. Part of me wanted to just end it then and there. For a casual relationship, it was already proving to be more emotionally taxing than I was prepared for, and with work ramping up, I couldn't afford any distractions.

But then I heard Ruth's words playing through my head. *"This sort of thing doesn't come along all that often."* That statement was truer than she'd realised. The chemistry between Sebastian and I was unlike anything I'd experienced before. It was practically nuclear. And he'd promised that there was so much more to learn.

I closed my eyes for a moment, collecting my thoughts. "Look Sebastian, I'm going to go out on a limb and guess most women you sleep with don't have a problem with this sort of arrangement. I bet they're pretty happy to take whatever you give them. But I'm not like that. I can't just be another pretty ornament."

"I never considered you to be," he replied, his expression earnest.

"Then start showing it. I'm happy to keep this relationship simple, but simple doesn't mean totally one dimensional. If we're going to continue, I need to feel like you're putting in at least a little effort. It doesn't have to be much, a quick bite to eat once every few weeks, a phone call or message now and then. If that's too much to ask, well, I'm sure you can find what you're looking for elsewhere."

He contemplated this. It didn't seem like I was asking much, but apparently it wasn't an easy decision.

"If that's what you need to feel comfortable, I'll do my best," he said eventually. "But in return, you have to understand that there are times I might not be able to contact you. I seek these sorts of relationships for a reason. It's true, I tend to keep my distance out of habit, even when I don't need to, but the fact remains that my schedule is incredibly unpredictable. I could be called to fly overseas tonight, and even when I am here, I'm often so busy I barely have time to eat or sleep."

I nodded. "I can sympathise with that." His words seemed fair. I knew the toll work could take on a person's personal relationships. Suddenly, I felt embarrassed at the way I'd reacted. He was just like me in a lot of ways; career driven and focused, almost to a fault. I could hardly hold that against him.

"I'm sorry too," I continued. "Maybe I overreacted. I'm not good at this stuff. I'm willing to compromise if you are."

"Sounds good to me," he said.

"Excellent." I still felt a little uneasy, but I'd said my piece and he seemed to have taken it to heart. I couldn't ask for more than that. "So why did you decide to pop in anyway? I assume it wasn't to get told off."

He smiled. "Actually I brought you something."

"Oh? Trying to bribe your way out of trouble then?"

"Not really. It's more of a return than a gift." He reached into his bag and pulled out the shoes I'd left on his office floor that first night we'd met. "I believe you were a little too pre-occupied to take them with you the other week."

I couldn't help but laugh. *So now he brings them.*

"Am I missing something?" he asked.

"Oh it's nothing," I said, suddenly aware of how childish

the story seemed.

"No, go on."

I sighed. "It's stupid really. Remember when I said I'd explain my safe word?" He nodded. "Well, when I was running away that first night, it occurred to me that the situation bore some passing similarity to Cinderella. You know, shoes left behind at the ball and all that."

He seemed to find this incredibly amusing. "I'm a little rusty with my fairy tales, but I don't remember Cinderella being quite as sordid as that particular evening."

"You mustn't have been reading the right version."

"Apparently not." He grinned. "Well, that does explain why you were in such a hurry to leave. And here I was thinking you were embarrassed."

I shook my head. "Nope. I just had to escape before pumpkin o'clock."

Sliding closer, he wrapped his arms around my hips, locking my body against his. "So if you're Cinderella, that makes me Prince Charming then?"

Whatever lingering frustration I'd felt instantly melted away. "I guess so," I said, my voice suddenly fluttering. *How the hell does he keep doing that to me?*

"Well then, I believe that means that since I've returned your lost slippers, we're meant to kiss now."

I knew I should probably stop him. Someone could walk in at any moment. But as usual, I seemed to have no willpower where he was concerned. Craning his neck, he brought his mouth down to meet mine. The kiss was somehow firm and hungry, yet impossibly soft, and the warmth of it flowed through me. As our bodies rocked back against my desk, he reached up and ran one hand roughly through my hair, driving us together, as though someone might steal me away at any moment.

Some indeterminable time later, he broke away. "I do believe I should bring you things more often," he said with a smile.

"I'm not sure I'd ever get much done if you did." Glancing and the clock I winced. "Speaking of getting things done, you should probably go. As much as I don't want to go back to this stuff, it'll just be there tomorrow if I don't do it today."

I slipped out from under his arms and reached to open the door, but he followed behind me, catching my wrist in his hand and sliding up against me until my body was pressed into the wood. Trapped again.

"I'm sorry we don't have more time," he said, drawing his free hand softly down my hip. "I do like the idea of fucking you right here."

I could feel his excitement jutting into my lower back like hot metal. *Just a few inches lower and... Jesus Sophia, you're at work for fuck's sake.*

"This is my office, Sebastian," I said, trying to sound disapproving. I didn't do a very good job.

Dropping his head down he brushed his lips gently across the curve of my neck. "Well, I guess that wouldn't be proper," he whispered. "We'll just have to wait. Are you free tomorrow night?"

"I think so."

"Good. Then come to the Royal Bay hotel, room four hundred, at eight o'clock."

"Why?"

"You said you wanted to start learning more about what it is to submit, so tomorrow I'm going to show you. I think you'll find the experience... eye opening." Releasing me, he took a step back and opened the door himself. "Until then, Sophia." And before I could muster a reply, he was gone.

I stood for a few moments trying to collect myself, his

final words still ringing in my ears. Last time we'd been to-gether, in the heat of the moment, I'd said that maybe I wanted to be shown something more, but now he'd called me on it. *Well what the hell did you think he'd do, missionary with the lights off forever?*

In spite of what his dominance did to me, I still had my doubts. There was a big difference between a bit of playful restraint and the sorts of things he enjoyed. Was I really one of those girls?

Apparently I was about to find out.

Chapter 11

The next morning I took a long shower and then ventured outside to find breakfast, looking forward to doing not much of anything. At the start of the year, I promised myself I'd take one Sunday a month off from work entirely. When you work for a big law firm, it's easy to lose all sense of balance. One day a month doesn't sound like much, but it's enough to feel like you've still got some semblance of control over your life.

I brought a book along with me. I used to love to read in high school, but with free time an ever shrinking commodity, my 'to read' pile kept growing faster than I could get through it. Those Sundays were about the only time I ever made any progress.

I leafed through a few pages, trying my best to concentrate, but my mind kept wandering back to Sebastian. It annoyed me. I wasn't the sort of girl who pined after men. For me, sex had always been just another fun way to pass the time. Except with Sebastian, it was something more.

I wasn't sure whether to be afraid or excited about the coming evening. He'd given me almost no clues about what to expect.

Almost.

That morning, I'd received a text message.

I want you to bring something with you tonight. A length of red ribbon, about three feet long.

I didn't know why he couldn't simply bring it himself, but at least I had some vague idea of what lay in store. As far as I could see, a ribbon could only be to bind me, so I knew I'd likely be restrained, but beyond that I was still in the dark. I suspected that was part of the experience. On the plus side, I now had his number.

I finished my breakfast, stubbornly forcing my way through a few chapters, before throwing in the towel. It was time to go shopping.

There was a fabric store just a few blocks from my place. It was a little strange to be hunting for something so kinky in such a mundane location. Sebastian had turned a simple act of shopping into something decidedly more sordid. As I walked the aisles, I found myself staring at the ground, trying my best not to meet the eyes of the other customers. It didn't help that the store seemed to be entirely populated by little old ladies. There was no way they could know why I was really there, but nonetheless, after I paid, I hustled out of the store as quickly as possible, burying the ribbon in the bottom of my bag.

The rest of the day passed at a snail's pace. I tried to enjoy my time off by catching up on some television I'd DVR'd, but I found it difficult to concentrate. I was nervous and buzzing with energy.

Seven thirty rolled around, and after finding nothing that screamed 'kinky hotel rendezvous' in my wardrobe, I threw on the closest thing I had — a bright red cocktail dress that flared at the bottom — and headed for Circular Quay once more. I was probably going to be early, but I got the impression that tardiness would not go down well tonight.

The hotel was only a minute's walk from the restaurant we'd been at a few weeks back. *A girl could get used to this kind of living*, I thought, as I walked along the wharf.

There was a storm rolling in from the south. The sky looked angry, bruised purple and swollen with rain; sea spray rode on the whipping wind. People seemed to have wisely taken the hint and stayed inside. Aside from a few gallant restaurant patrons, the area was largely empty.

The Royal Bay was a deceptively simple looking building. Unlike most city hotels, it was only a few stories tall, and the warm glow that trickled from the windows lent it a homely feel. But sitting on the docks, just meters from the water, it was definitely a step up from the Holiday Inn.

"Hi," I said to the elegant middle aged woman behind the reception desk, "I'm here to meet a friend of mine. He said to come to room 400."

Her smile wavered for the briefest instant before returning to full strength. *Shit.* It hadn't occurred to me before, but sexed up like I was and visiting an unnamed male guest in his room alone, I realised what I looked like. *Yep, lawyer by day, high class hooker by night. That's me.* I could have laughed if I wasn't so mortified.

"Of course, just take the lift over there up to the fourth floor. It's the first door on your right."

"Great, thanks," I said, doing my best to keep my expression neutral. Trying to correct her seemed like more trouble than it was worth.

As the lift gradually ticked its way upwards, my nerves continued to build. In the past, my sexual encounters had always been vaguely predictable. Even when the relationship was new, I had some idea what to expect. It was still exciting, but there was a comfort in that familiarity. With Sebastian, however, I was going in blind. The whole thing was a mystery.

With my heart thumping, I made my way slowly down the corridor until I found the room. Taking a deep breath, I knocked twice. There was no response. I tried again with the same result. Had I gotten mixed up somehow? I was fairly sure I had the details right, but Sebastian didn't strike me as the flaky sort. Not knowing what else to do, I reached out tentatively and tugged on the heavy brass handle. The door fell open without a sound.

At first I thought I was in the wrong place. The lights were dim and the room appeared to be empty. I made my way inside, glancing around nervously like a girl in a horror film, but Sebastian was nowhere in sight.

The room was stunning. Decked in soft creams and whites, it offered the kind of open space most hotel guests could only dream of. In front of the giant king sized bed was a rolling window that opened directly on to a balcony, offering me a perfect panoramic view of the harbour. I gazed out for several seconds, watching a lightning bolt sear the sky a blinding white. The storm was drawing closer.

It wasn't until I spotted the envelope that I realised I hadn't messed up. It was resting on a chair in the middle of the room. *Oh so that's how we're playing is it?* A thrill surged through me as I approached.

There was something else sitting beside it; a strip of dark silk about as long as my arm. I picked it up, running its softness through my fingers and trying to imagine what it was for. More restraints? Or something more sensual?

The whole situation had a clandestine flavour to it. The dark room, the mysterious props, the secret instructions, they all made me feel incredibly naughty; like I was doing something much more illicit than simply having sex.

Written on the front of the envelope was a single word. 'Sophia'. There was something about the way he said my name that carried more weight than normal. I found myself hearing the word in his voice as I read it.

Inside was a simple set of instructions:

Sophia.

I'm happy you could join me. I think you will find tonight's activities most enlightening. To prepare, I want you to strip down to your panties. I trust you've discovered the blindfold I left for you. Once you're undressed, stand in the middle of the room. Place the ribbon I asked for on the bed next to you and then cover your eyes with the scarf. Wait like that until I come for you.

-S

I picked up the silk gingerly and held it up to the light. It was completely opaque. Once it was secured in place, I'd be utterly blind. He'd be able to do whatever he wanted and I wouldn't even see it coming. The thought made me tremble.

For the hundredth time I considered calling it off. He'd promised to leave me alone if that was what I wanted. All I had to do was turn around and walk out of the door and everything would return to normal.

Except I knew that wasn't really true.

The fire that had been lit inside me wouldn't just disappear. As frightening as the thought of presenting myself for him - exposed, blind and helpless - was, the alternative was even more so. For better or for worse, I had to know.

I began to strip off, folding my clothes neatly on the bed, before pulling the ribbon from my purse. Just looking at it again made me blush. Mindful of my skin, I'd bought the softest, lightest weave I could find. I played with it for a few seconds, winding it around my wrists, trying to imagine what it would feel like to be bound with it, before placing it on the bed too.

I fidgeted for a few more moments, ensuring everything was in order, but eventually I knew I was just making excuses. *Christ, here goes nothing.* Picking up the blindfold, I gazed at the room one final time, before slipping it over my head and knotting it at the back. Everything went black.

My pulse instantly quickened. Stripping off my clothes was something I did every day. It hadn't felt unusual. But the second I covered my eyes, I'd crossed a line into the unknown. Anything could happen now.

We'd begun.

I wasn't sure how long I stood there. Unable to see, time seemed to slow down. Every tiny hotel noise made me jump, and my mind was racing at a million miles a minute. Was he even coming at all? Maybe this was a test of some sort, to see how long I'd stay put. And if he did show, could I ask him to remove the blindfold? It really was terrifying, but that might be against the rules. I didn't even know what the rules were. Was I allowed to object? Oh Christ, what the hell was I doing?

"Hello Sophia," said a voice from behind me.

I squealed in surprise. He'd made no noise, nothing to give himself away. He must have been hiding in the bathroom the whole time, simply watching and letting me stew.

"Hello," I managed.

"I'm very happy you didn't have a change of heart. I think we're both going to have a lot of fun."

"That's easy for you to say, you're not naked and blind."

He laughed. "Believe me, that's just the beginning."

Being unable to see made me incredibly tense. I had no idea what was going on around me. He could have filled the room with a live studio audience and I wouldn't have known. My muscles were tight with anticipation, my body primed, although for what I wasn't certain.

His voice moved around me in a slow orbit. "I didn't really get to look at you the other night. Things were a little... rushed." I flinched as a hand trailed across my stomach, moving tantalisingly close to my breasts. "God, you're gorgeous. You look every bit as ravishing as I expected."

There was something vaguely dirty about being ogled so openly by a virtual stranger, but part of me was enjoying the attention.

"Are you afraid?"

I hesitated, before nodding slowly.

"That's okay. But don't worry; I'll take care of you." His voice was soft now, and it hovered just inches from my ear, the heat of his breath tickling my neck. "We both know you want this as much as I do. You need this."

And despite all of my apprehensions, I knew he was right. I couldn't help but think back to the previous night when he'd pinned me down. The surge of adrenaline, the primal need that had seized me in that moment, was unlike anything I'd experienced before. I had to have that again.

"I know," I said, my voice barely more than a whisper.

His hands continued to traverse my body, gently teasing my back, my arms, the slope of my neck. He never stayed in one spot for very long, pulling away before surprising me from another angle. Every stroke left my skin tingling. In the darkness, the tension inside me grew. On some level I knew this was part of the game, drawing things out until I was at breaking point, but it was hard to be rational in such a position.

Eventually I felt him slide in behind me. "Are you ready to begin?"

I swallowed loudly. *Last chance, Sophia.* But there was no

going back now.

"Yes."

"Good. Then put your hands behind your back, arms together."

Shaking, I did as I was told. I stood there, waiting to feel the soft touch of the ribbon, but instead something slick and fibrous wrapped around my wrists.

"What about the ribbon?" I blurted out.

"What about it?" he replied, looping and tying off the rope. "I never told you what it was for. Don't worry; we'll make good use of it later."

I took a deep breath and tried to rein in my pounding heartbeat. "This just isn't what I expected."

He gave a little laugh. "The game's no fun if it's predictable Sophia. And on that note..."

Before I knew what had happened, another length of rope was passed around my ankles. I cried out in alarm.

He worked quickly, and in a matter of seconds my legs were pinned as tightly as my arms. "Perfect," he said.

Instinctively I tried to wriggle free and nearly fell over in the process. A wave of panic washed over me. Trying to remain calm, I tested my bonds more carefully, but it quickly became obvious that there was no way out. The knots were firm, the pressure high enough to restrict mobility while not being painful or dangerous. He was clearly a master of his craft. I was held as thoroughly as any prisoner.

I came incredibly close to just ending it there. My safe word sat on the tip of my tongue. But I managed to subdue my fear. *Harden up, Sophia. This is what you signed up for, remember?*

I'd been expecting him to bind me. That was BDSM 101. I just hadn't realised how thorough he'd be. I'd had this image in my mind of being playfully tied down, able to escape but choosing not to. The reality was far more intense. I couldn't move. I might have been able to hop to the door given time, but I wasn't even sure what direction it was in, anymore. He could now do anything he wanted to me. I was totally at his mercy. It was as exhilarating as it was terrifying. Like the help-lessness of the previous night, but a hundred times stronger.

The rope also surprised me. If the ribbon wasn't to hold me, then what was it for? What other surprises did he have planned? The only certainty I had left was that I was com-pletely in his hands.

A low rumble resonated from his throat. "I haven't been able to stop thinking about this all day. Our night together was amazing, but it wasn't enough. I need to have you all. For tonight, Sophia, you're mine."

I nodded, not trusting myself to speak.

Hands encircled my body. "I want to hear you say it."

"I'm yours," I said, my voice quaking. There was a sense of finality about that statement that echoed within me long after the words were gone.

"Louder."

"I'm yours," I said more steadily.

He purred softly against my neck. "And I plan to take full advantage."

I suppressed a squeal as his powerful arms wrapped around me and scooped me into the air. For the second time in as many days he carried me across the room and lay me gently on the bed.

"God you look sexy, all tied up for me."

The mattress shifted under his weight as he straddled me, and then his lips were on mine. The kiss was strong and ur-gent, and my body turned to liquid beneath it. His tongue slipped into my mouth, exploring, teasing, exciting, while his hands found their way to my chest.

"I've been waiting to play with these since the first time I saw you," he said, squeezing my breasts gently. Wrapping his lips around one nipple, he flicked his tongue over the hardened peak before circling the areola lazily. I arched beneath him, stretching against my bonds, powerless to the pleasure that was coursing through me.

Unlike our last encounter, he took his time. He worked his way down slowly, stroking and kissing every part of me as if claiming uncharted territory. Places that had never seemed sexy to me lit up under his touch, leaving me a trembling, panting mess.

By the time he reached the top of my panties, I was soaking wet. Every touch of his tongue seemed like a promise.

"Fuck, you smell so good," he said, his lips softly caressing my thighs. "But tonight you have to earn that kind of pleasure. From now on, you aren't allowed to come until I say so. Understand? Your orgasms are mine."

I moaned in protest.

"Good things come to those who wait," he chided. "Right now I want to see your ass."

He climbed off me, slid his hands underneath my body and turned me over. With my wrists bound behind me, I had nothing to rest on at the front, which left me kneeling at an angle, my head resting on a pillow and my bottom jutting out into the air.

He made an appreciative sound. "Fuck, it's perfect," he said, stroking me roughly. There was something in the way he touched me there that made my stomach tighten. It conjured memories of Hannah bent over the desk awaiting her punishment. I had an uneasy feeling I knew what came next.

"You know, we still haven't dealt with your little penchant for teasing," he said, as if on cue, punctuating the statement with a single gentle smack.

I tried to recoil, but there was nowhere to go. "I'm not sure... I mean..." but I couldn't get the words out. The conservative part of my mind was screaming at the indecency of what was about to happen, but the deeper I went down the rabbit hole, the more muffled that voice got. The whole thing felt unavoidable. There I was, bound, bent and blindfolded in front of a man I barely knew, my skin hot, my body flushed with hormones. He'd told me he'd stop if I gave the word, but at that point I wasn't really sure if that was true. What was scarier was that I didn't know if I wanted him to.

"Shh, shh," he said. "It's your first time. I'll be gentle."

Before I could complain, he swept me up in his arms again and spun me around until I came to rest over his knee. The ease with which he could manipulate me was a huge turn on. Even if I wasn't bound, I couldn't have stopped him.

He tugged my panties together in the middle, exposing more of my skin to the air. "Now this will sting at first. Give it a chance. Try to embrace it. Pain and pleasure are closer than most people realise." He rubbed my ass tenderly. "Are you ready?"

I quivered. I didn't know if I'd ever be ready. But nonetheless I found myself nodding.

With my eyes covered, I couldn't even see it coming. One second his hand was resting lightly against me, the next it was crashing into my left cheek. The pain was hot and sharp and instant, like a tiny explosion against my skin. I grunted through gritted teeth.

The blows began to fall in a steady rhythm. There was no conversation, just the meaty crack of flesh on flesh. At first, I felt nothing but pain. My skin burned under the onslaught, and every slap seemed to sting a little more than the last.

But as my body adjusted, a strange sense of peace began to settle over me. Each smack was as inevitable as the last, so rather than shy away, I did as he'd suggested. I began to embrace them. They still stung on a physical level, but gradually I began to realise that there was more to the experience than just pain.

My skin had grown more sensitive than I'd ever thought possible, and every touch sent waves of sensation rolling through me. Pain and pleasure wound themselves together, until it was difficult to see where one ended and the other began. It was an exhilarating combination.

There was also something incredibly erotic about being turned over Sebastian's knee, having him do those things to me. With the ropes, I'd given control over to him, and now he was exercising it. The intense display of dominance I'd witnessed while crouched in the wardrobe was now directed at me. And it felt fantastic. The simple satisfaction of complete submission.

Again, Sebastian showed an uncanny ability to read me. "You see? It feels good doesn't it?"

"Yes," I replied. And I meant it.

Feeling more confident, I began to experiment. I shifted against him, lining my crotch up with the curve of his thigh. The next blow caused them to grind together, chasing the pain with a tremor of ecstasy. My cries began to dissolve into moans as the line blurred even further.

With the last of my resistance bleeding away, everything began to take on a new dimension. The ropes that I'd struggled so hard against became exciting in their strength. My blindness, once terrifying, now amplified every sensation. I was no longer afraid to discover what wicked secrets Sebastian had planned; I was excited.

He paused and ran his hands lightly over my burning flesh, soothing it in small circles. "Mmm, cherry red. I love a good spanking. I'm not really much of a sadist as far as doms go — whips and chemicals are a bit beyond me — but the sight of a girl bent over my knee, red ass in the air, just drives me wild."

His fingers slid down and slipped inside my panties, parting them to one side, causing me to moan in anticipation. "It looks like I'm not the only one who enjoyed that," he said, running his fingers slowly up my slit. "It's a pity you can't feel how wet you are for yourself. But I think I can do one better."

There was a pulling sensation against my legs and a loud rip. He'd torn my panties free! I opened my mouth to object, but before I got out so much as a word, he crammed them between my lips.

"You were wondering what the ribbon was for," he said, as I felt something soft loop around my head. "Well now you know. I want you to taste yourself, to taste how wet I made you. I want you to understand how much you enjoyed getting bound and spanked."

The scent of my arousal was almost overpowering. It filled my nostrils and rolled down my throat. He was right; I'd never been so turned on before.

He tied the ribbon off behind my head. "Perfect."

With the gag in place, my helplessness grew. One by one, my freedoms were being stolen away. I couldn't move, I couldn't see, and now I couldn't even talk properly. He'd reduced me to little more than a life-sized doll that he could pose and play with however he wished.

"Seeing as your mouth is currently occupied, if you want me to stop at any point, clap your hands. Understand?"

It hadn't occurred to me that my safe word would be useless, but once again his experience shone through. I nodded.

"Excellent. You know, you're doing so well, I think you've earned a reward."

I nodded again eagerly. My whole body ached for him,

begging to be satisfied.

For a few agonising seconds nothing happened. I began to think maybe he had another surprise in store, but then his finger was pushing into me. I moaned into the gag.

"Fuck, you're so wet for me," he said, slipping past my folds with liquid smoothness. "I love that I can do this to you. You have no idea how hard it makes me, seeing you like this."

I made a noise, something between a cry and a plea. His finger felt amazing, but it wasn't enough. I needed more. I bucked against him, pushing him deeper, and he responded, siding in to the lowest knuckle and crooking his finger in a 'come hither' gesture that made my insides melt.

"God, you're greedy tonight aren't you? Well, I've never been one to turn down an invitation." A second finger joined the first, stretching me wider, while the rough pad of his thumb found my clit and began to work it in slow circles.

I knew I wouldn't last long. The night's intricate, sensuous torture had my body humming just millimetres below the edge. I braced myself against his legs, preparing for that sweet release to come tearing through me.

But right as I was on the brink, he pulled away.

"Now, now," he said over my wordless protests, "remember what I said earlier? You can't come without permission. Your orgasms are mine."

He set me down on my knees on the bed. There was a rustling of material, but I barely noticed, too focused on the pleasure inside me that was slowly ebbing away. I'd been so close!

"You know with a lot of practice, I may be able to teach you to come for me on command," he said, stroking my back soothingly. "I gave one girl a screaming orgasm in a crowded mall with just simple instructions. It's amazing what people are capable of when they truly surrender themselves."

It sounded ridiculous. Orgasms were hard enough to achieve the regular way. I doubted any level of submission would change that.

"I know you probably don't believe me. It's true, you're a long way from being able to do that, but you might be closer than you think."

His fingers wrapped tightly around my hips as he leaned in close. "Now I want you to come for me," he growled, and with a single violent thrust he rammed his cock inside me.

The effect was instantaneous. My orgasm roared back to life, exploding through my body in a surge of muscle curling warmth. The breath drained from my lungs as my pussy clenched tight around his hardness, until I was sure I must be hurting him. It was the most intense orgasm of my life.

"You see, you might be capable of more than you think."

As my body convulsed one final time, I couldn't help but agree. I had a lot to learn about myself.

"I'm not done with you yet," he said. "Christ, you feel good. You're wet enough to take all of me already." To prove his point he thrust himself deep, burying his shaft all the way to the root. I moaned with the size of him.

With no need to ease into it, the animal took over. He drove himself into me with a bestial urgency. One hand fell onto my back, pushing me into the bed, while the other seized my shoulder, grinding me against him in time with his thrusts.

I had never felt so utterly possessed before. In that moment, bound and held, I was his, every part of me, to tease and touch and fuck as he wished. I wasn't sure I'd ever get enough of that feeling.

His pace slowed and I felt his hand slide up to the back of my head.

"I think it's time to remove these," he said, fingering the

blindfold and ribbon. "I want you to see how you look trussed up for me. I want you to watch me as I fuck you."

He gave a tug and they both fell to the floor. The room sprang into view. It was strange being able to see again. For a second I merely blinked, struggling to get my bearings. Then my eyes fell on the mirror that occupied the far wall.

"You see now what you've let me do to you?" he asked. "And this is just the beginning. I can show you a whole world of pleasure just like this."

The image of my bound body being mounted from behind was almost too much. Sebastian had shed his clothes. He stood behind me naked, taut, and glistening with sweat. A pure, primal picture of masculinity. It was the first time I'd seen him fully undressed. There was barely an ounce of fat on him. From his perfectly toned biceps to his powerful chest to the magnificent V of muscle that hugged his pelvis, the sight of him took my breath away.

I watched with wild eyes as that magnificent cock disappeared inside me, his body quivering with barely restrained ferocity. My ass glowed red in the lamplight, still raw from our earlier games, and every thrust sent a little sting coursing through me, as his stomach brushed that tender skin.

"Yes," I moaned, "I want you to show me."

Shifting angles, he brought his hand up to my ass, his fingers playing gently across the delicate, rosy ring at the centre. Under other circumstances I'd probably have been shocked by that alien sensation, but as excited as I was, I took it in stride.

"Have you ever let a man fuck you here?" he asked, lubing himself with my juices and pushing just the tiniest way inside me. I felt an unexpected thread of pleasure shoot through me.

"No," I replied. "I've done a little anal play, but it was a long time ago."

116

"Then we'll go slow," he said. "But I want to have you there eventually. I want to have you everywhere, Sophia. Every part of you is mine." There was no question in his voice, and I didn't object. I knew it was true. Besides, of all the things I'd let him do, this seemed almost tame by comparison.

His breathing began to quicken. I could hear it in his sounds, those raw, animal grunts; he was getting close.

"I want you to come with me, Sophia. I want to feel you tighten around me as I blow inside you."

"Oh god, oh fuck," I cried, already well past the point of no return.

"Now Sophia, I'm coming!"

I'd always thought simultaneous orgasms were a phenomenon reserved for porn and cheap romance novels, but Sebastian seemed to be making it a mission to show me how much I didn't know. We rocked together, our bodies writhing in ecstatic unison as our climaxes took hold. There was an incredible sense of connection in that moment, like we were sharing one orgasm that burst outward into both of us. He buried himself inside me almost to the point of pain, and I pushed back, my whole body clenching and tingling.

When it was over, we both fell boneless and breathless to the bed. For a while we just dozed in silence, content to bask in the glow of what had just happened. It seemed like I should say something, but I wasn't sure I could put into words what I was feeling at that moment.

My arms and legs were still bound, but I didn't mind. Lying there with one of his powerful arms wrapped around me, I felt completely safe.

"That was wonderful," he said, sometime later.

I nodded and let out a little sigh.

He reached up and began to unbind me. "You're a natural submissive, you know that? I know you were afraid, but once we began, you were perfect."

"I didn't know being tied up was considered a skill."

He laughed. It was a big, boisterous sound that shook the bed beneath me. "Don't think of it as a skill. Think of it as a mindset. It takes a lot of courage to give yourself to someone like that. Not everyone can do it."

"I guess so." A shiver rolled down my spine as I thought back on all the things I'd just let him do. "To be honest, it wasn't really what I was expecting," I continued. "Even after the other night, part of me still thought it would feel... wrong somehow. Like I was being exploited."

He nodded slowly. "Society has a lot of misconceptions about what we do. That's one of the big ones. Don't get me wrong, there are plenty of guys out there who use it as an excuse to abuse women, but that's not what submission is really about. A true dom only has as much control as their partner allows. It's a gift given from one person to another, and don't think for one second I'm not thankful for that."

"Well, you're welcome," I replied, feeling a little bewildered by his words. "I hadn't really thought of it that way before, but it makes me feel better knowing you're not just waiting for the right moment to chain me to the bed and never let me leave."

"Only if you give me permission," he said with a grin.

"I'll keep that in mind."

A few minutes later, he drifted off. I tried to join him, but sleep wouldn't come. My mind was spinning, still trying to process all the new sensations and emotions that were swirling inside me.

I no longer had any doubt that Sebastian was right. I was a submissive. The way my body turned to hot clay in his hands was proof enough of that. But I had to be careful. I couldn't let myself get in too deep. It was hard not to feel some kind of connection when you gave yourself to somebody so completely like that, but the fact was that this was just business as usual for him. Something fun to pass the time. Letting myself believe it was anything else was dangerous. All I could do was enjoy it for what it was.

After another twenty minutes of tossing and turning, I decided that maybe I needed a little help shutting down. Slipping out from under the covers I headed over to the mini bar. The tiny bottle of champagne was thirty dollars, but given the rate for the room was almost certainly more than my monthly rent, I figured Sebastian wouldn't mind.

I'd been so drained by what we'd done, I'd had no time to look at the aftermath, but standing there in the moonlight, gazing at the scattered clothing, underwear, and kinky paraphernalia that littered the floor, I couldn't help but smile. If anyone were to burst in at that moment they'd have no trouble guessing what we'd been up to.

Surveying the room really highlighted how impressive it was. I made pretty good money, and was no stranger to splurging on the occasional fancy hotel when I felt like a treat, but this was unlike anything I'd ever seen. It made me wonder again about the man I'd tangled myself up with. I knew that kind of wanton disregard for money was common amongst the super-rich, and although I'd had my suspicions, he'd had answers to all of my questions. It should have been enough, but I still couldn't shake the feeling that there was something more to him than that.

Then again, perhaps I was just being paranoid. I had no illusions about my trust issues, and I didn't put it past my subconscious to try and sabotage a good thing before it could hurt me.

My reverie was interrupted by a buzzing sound behind me. Turning, I discovered that Sebastian had left his phone on the counter above the bar. The screen was lit up with a text message that had just arrived. My eyes ran over it before I could stop them. It took me a few seconds to process what I saw.

His wallpaper was a picture of a girl. Slim and blonde with a stunningly beautiful face, she wore one of those serene smiles that screams 'young and in love.' I felt a pang of jealousy gazing at those perfect features.

But it was the text message that had just arrived which really caught my eye.

Still thinking of you. Call me.

The number was not a listed contact, but there was an accompanying attachment. With shaking fingers I scooped it up and tapped the screen to open it, and a naked female body appeared before me. Her head wasn't visible, but her open legs and seductive pose left little doubt as to her intentions.

Nausea twisted my stomach, and the phone fell from my hand. I couldn't believe it. I'd just let Sebastian tie me up and do unspeakable things to me, and he'd been lying all along. My first instinct had been right. He wasn't any different, just another guy who would say and do whatever it took to get a girl into bed, and I'd fallen for it hook line and sinker. Who knew how many other women there were right now.

I suddenly felt dirty. Used. Nothing more than another water cooler story for the office next week.

Before I knew it, I was out the door, and then stumbling through the lobby. There was a different woman behind the counter now, younger and kinder looking. She gave me a sympathetic smile as I stormed past. It didn't surprise me. I was probably quite a sight. With my hair a mess, my makeup smeared, and my dress unfastened, I probably looked the epitome of a jilted lover.

Outside the storm had passed, leaving the ground slick and the air sharp. I wrapped my arms around myself to try and ward off the chill. It was late and I was a long way from my house, but I stubbornly ignored the taxis driving past. I couldn't stomach the idea of being around anyone at that moment.

The entire way home one thought just kept playing through my mind. *How could I have been so stupid?*

About the Author

Maya Cross is a writer who enjoys making people blush. Growing up with a mother who worked in a book store, she read a lot from a very young age, and soon enough picked up a pen of her own. She's tried her hands at a whole variety of genres including horror, science fiction, and fantasy, but funnily enough, it was the sexy stuff that stuck. She has now started this pen name as an outlet for her spicier thoughts (they were starting to overflow). She likes her heroes strong but mysterious, her encounters sizzling, and her characters true to life.

She believes in writing familiar narratives told with a twist, so most of her stories will feel comfortable, but hopefully a little unique. Whatever genre she's writing, finding a fascinating concept is the first and most important step.

The Alpha Group is her first attempt at erotic romance.

When she's not writing, she's playing tennis, trawling her home town of Sydney for new inspiration, and drinking too much coffee.

Website: http://www.mayacross.com
Facebook: http://facebook.com/mayacrossbooks
Twitter: https://twitter.com/Maya_cross

18274829R00080

Made in the USA
San Bernardino, CA
10 January 2015